PLAYIN'
4 KEEPS

TARIK

ABOUT THE AUTHOR

Tarik is the CEO of Fed Pen Publications and Reel Street Productions. He has authored six novels and has written three screenplays to date. He is currently incarcerated at the McDowell Federal Correctional Institution, where he awaits his anticipated release in 2024.

ACKNOWLEDGMENTS

First off, I would like to give all praise and thanks to the greatest author the creator of all that exists, Allah. Without whom none of this would be possible. To my mother, Linda who always encouraged me to read and bragged to her friends about my high reading scores in grade school. I finally did something with that, Ma. I love you stay healthy and strong. I'm blessed to have you as a mom. To my deceased father who passed down to me his stubborn will, love you, you are missed. I'm still trying to turn all that stubborn will into determination to succeed.

To my daughter, Rika I know I can be pushy and bossy sometimes, especially when I got a vision. Just know you can see your dreams better than other people can. You're headed for success, so you're going to figure that one out yourself. I love you! Thank you for being my hands and feet when I couldn't use my own. To my sister, T'yoshi, you are beautiful, creative, driven, and strong. I love you and thank you for helping me share my thoughts and ideas with the world. Now, secure the bag! Special one for my nieces and nephews. Unk loves y'all.

Tremell, thanks for the push at the end. It helped me get to the streets...keep up the hustle. I love you, Aunty Judy and Uncle Samir. Y'all assistance and support have been unwavering. Y'all always down like two flat tires against any dark road and I'm blessed to have y'all. To my cousin, Lawrence, what you did in the game was legendary. Now get out there and turn that shit into a legacy. Thank you for the hard street lessons you taught me. It is from you that I learned to hustle and play for keeps, to go for mines, and not to busy myself watching another nigga's pockets. Much love!

To Dirt, keep striving to reach that mighty goal. Those who touch their lowest low always reach their highest heights. To Hunky B, Whitey, Super Lou. Thank y'all for the chisels y'all used on me as a shorty. That shit hurt like a muhfucka, but it left some shit etched in. Much love to all y'all. D- Stone, stay healthy and stay strong, much love. To my nigga, Main. I know I be blowing you, Joe. But I'm a man of strong convictions just like you. Thanks for being there when I need you. That's hard to come by. I recognize that. Much love and a bunch of one hunnids.

To, Jayball, Tobe, Wook, The Pound, 38th Street, The Block Continues. Much love. To Rondell, Dread, Mick-Stone. Much love and lots of one hunnids. To Reesie-Bo, R-Jay...Much love, y'all. To T-Man...much love, keep striving to get out. To my Muslim brotha Hasan (Craig) that love runs deep. You ain't missed a beat. Thanks for the love and support. I saw what they did to nephew. Some niggas just too real for the rap game. Rest in peace King Von. O'Block Y'all lost a real one. To Big Laid, since day one you be striving at that music shit, I remember you was DJ'ing and rapping in your old G Garage, keep workin' Joe, You're almost there. Much love thanks for the support.

To 39th Street. The Ida B. Wells Housing Projects much love to all y'all. They gon' remember we was there. The Stateway Gardens. The Robert Taylors. The Ickies PC's. The Bungalows. Newtown, Fifthward, The Cabrini Greens. What's up Lil Nut? Much love. To all organizations, The illustrious Black Disciple Nation, Much love. The Gangster Disciples, The Black Peace Stones, The Vice Lords, The Latin Folks, The Latin Kings much love. To the Crips and Bloods East Coast, West Coast. Dirty South. To the Trenches of America and all over the world, much love. I'm pulling for y'all to make it out. Where y'all at ain't a bad place to begin a journey, it's just a bad place to get stuck, y'all know what I'm saying?

To all the Muslims, if y'all know anything about me, y'all know I'm working my way toward the Islamic Da'wah. Bear with me as I bring the trenches with me. To my bro, Homi-Has, Erie Ave, Vanango...stand up! You're so North Philly, Ock. Thanks for the push when I was stuck being my own worst critic much love. Big Troy West Philly, stand up you 'bout to get your shot, Bull. Don't shot a brick, Ock, that shit will build another wall for you. To Baseer, Wasim, and Bo from Wilmington, DE, Salams, and much love. Wasim and Bo are to dope authors check them out. To my DC Ock, King Reek, Southeast, 37th Street, Glizzy Gang stand up! Y'all pick up that King of the Yo. When real niggas writing about the trenches real niggas gotta support 'em. Much love and thanks for the point and the right direction.

To my Cellie 7 Mile Black, Westside D-town stand up, Boy...in my Big Sean voice. Thanks for listening as I worked my way through these plots with the light on all night. Much love. To Suit and Ty, your slow typing ass burnt through all my trulincs. Thanks for finally helping me get this draft to the editor much love. To Dynasty Visionary Designs, Thanks for helping me bring my dream cover to cover, into reality much love and success in the future. FCI Pekin, FCI Bennettsville, USP Atwater, USP Allenwood, USP Leavenworth, All of the BOP, I'm trying to get y'all out of there for a minute much love.

Rest in Peace to my Fam, Sohn, Shavell, Chuck, y'all gone but not forgotten. Rest in Peace Pooh-dog, Bean(ugly), Lil Mike y'all gone but not forgotten. Shout out to 300, 600, O'Block, Lowend, Englewood, Woodlawn, Eastside, Westside, The Wild 100's, Dixmoor, and Harvey, Much love. Dolton, Cal City, Shout out to everybody who supports me and black authors. Chi' Raq, ATL, NYC, LA, Detriot, B-More, Philly, DC, Memphis, Chat-Town. To all the real niggas all over the world, if I didn't mention you by name or your set, this your time to shine, Joe_____

Hope I left you enough space. Fill your name in on the line.

To my readers, My new Playin' 4 Keeps Fam. Part 2 is on the way. The sequel Scars for Scabs gets deeper. Thanks for trusting me to take y'all on this journey from Chi-Town 2 Chiraq and much love to y'all.

PLAYIN' 4 KEEPS

To play for keeps is to understand the seriousness of the moment and to meet it head-on, seizing its opportunities at all cost. When you play for keeps you use every talent, every gift, and every skill at your disposal to acquire whatever it is you may desire. People who play for keeps don't quit playing until they've won, no matter the manner of the obstacle, no matter the manner of setback. To play for keeps means you keep going, persevering against any kind of resistance, and you destroy anything in the path of your forward progress. Playing for keeps is a mindset, a concept, and a psychological roadmap. For those whose most passionate dream is to achieve.

CHAPTER 1
REGGIE WADE

"A'ight muhfuckas! Right now, this just a stick-up! It'll be on y'all if it turns into an ambulance pick-up!"

Everybody in the dim building lobby was caught with their pants down around their ankles. The vics froze in place and became a still picture of a gang of young niggas serving dope to fiends. Fear and surprise were in their eyes. I got the impression they were thinking that the very thing they thought would never happen to them was happening. *It was.*

I stared at the vics down the barrel of *The Beast*. The Beast is my sawed-off, double-barrel shotgun. She got a couple of scars and scrapes, but she still hurt pretty good. She's a scary bitch. Havin' a big gun in a stick-up do all the heavy liftin'. But when The Beast lost a vic's attention, I let that bitch blow and graffiti the walls with blood and guts. I don't play games, I play for keeps. I live on the edge. I need to find a less dangerous hustle. It's a fact out here that the stick-up man ain't got a long career. But what the fuck else am I gon' do?

I could sell drugs, try my hand at the con game, scamming. Them are all viable hustles, but they take too fucking long. I need mine and I need mine fast, like yesterday. I ain't got time to wait. I gotta have it cause I got habits. I snort dope, I smoke coke and squares, and I drink like a dry sponge. All that shit ain't gon' buy itself and I ain't a rich nigga, so...to make a short story even shorter, I'm the nigga on the dark street that asks you for a light. I'm the nigga standing beside yo' car when you stumble out of the club drunk. I'm the last nigga these dope dealers wanna see. I make a muhfucka low' me that shit like they owe me that shit. Fuck these niggas! They ain't cut from the same cloth I'm cut from anyway. Might as well run me that shit. Better me than them people. Straight like that.

Focused on the stain at hand, I reached into the pocket of my black trench coat, pulled out a black trash bag, and dropped it on the floor. The vics looked at the bag, then looked back at me, I think they was tryna' figure out what the trash bag was for. They didn't have to figure long.

I told them, "One at a time, I want all you muhfuckas to strip and put y'all shit—" I pointed The Beast down at the garbage bag. "—in that bag. No holdin' out on me. No cuffin'. Don't die over no material shit you can get back."

I swung The Beast back up and moved it left and right. Then I stopped the barrel at the chest of the first young nigga on the right. He was a baby nigga, couldn't have been no more than twelve or thirteen, but he had frizzy cornrows and dark lips that made him look like he drank hard liquor and smoked too much weed. Drugging out here in these streets makes a nigga look twice his age. The harder the drugs, the older a nigga looks. The drugs got harder...they always did...the longer a nigga stayed in the streets.

I told him, "You first, shorty. Show everybody how it's done."

He pouted, but he started stripping. He was young, but he wasn't a young fool. One by one all the vics started stripping and dropping all their shit into the bag. I never relaxed during a stick-up. Just as soon as everything was going right, in an instant, it could pivot on its heels and go left. A stick-up is like standing on the slippery lip of a skyscraper's roof. The slightest wind could blow and send you plunging to yo' death. Niggas tried shit, it wasn't smart. But niggas tried shit. So, I had a rule I robbed by, always keep full control. If I lose control, a nigga loses his life. Straight like that.

In seconds, the majority of the vics in the lobby were down to skin and dicks. I had the joint lookin' like an orgy in progress. The last nigga, a fat muhfucka with tits like a bitch, dropped his shit in the bag. But just as he did this, he cut his eye at me with a salty look on his grill, muggin' me on some tough shit. That pissed me off.

I swung The Beast left and stopped it at his chest. "Bitch ass nigga!" I snapped. "You got somethin' you wanna say to me?"

His chest lifted up. I had to give it to the fat muhfucka, he had heart. He faced me down and said, "You know who spot you robbin'?"

I almost spit in the nigga's face for askin' me that shit. He acted like I was supposed to. Or should be scared of the nigga he was referring to. I came out of a bag on his ass, "Vic, you know who robbin 'the spot?"

Fat boy threw his hands up like he was copping deuces. "I'm just sayin'...Dontae gon' be on yo' ass about this shit."

I gritted on the nigga. "Who the fuck is Dontae?"

Fat boy told me, "Bomb in a bag his shit and he ain't goin' for a nigga takin' nothin' from him."

"Oh, yeah?" I said, nodding my head slowly. "Is that right? Well,...I tell you what, vic. When you see Dontae tell him Reggie Wade said..."

Boom!

Before I realized it, I finger-fucked The Beast. That happened sometimes. Sometimes she begged me to fingerfuck her. She and my trigger finger had a relationship all of their own. The slug slammed into fat boy's chest, lifted him off his feet like he was levitating, and sent him flying back into the brick wall behind him. Slowly, his limp body slid to the floor, leaving a trail of thick-red blood. The rest of the vics chin was on the floor. The thunderous explosion was still echoing in the lobby. The pungent odor of gunpowder mixed with blood and guts floated in the air. I felt my dick get hard.

"Fuck Dontae!" I shouted. "Do I look like I give a fuck about Dontae?"

Left and right, I swung The Beast glarin' at the vics grimly down its scarred barrel. Shock and fear paralyzed them. I took the opportunity to swoop in, scoop up the trash bag and throw it over my shoulder.

"Who else got some shit to say? Anybody else got some shit they wanna say to me!" I yelled.

A bunch of heads shook at the same time.

Dontae.

I'd never heard the name. I been in these Ida B. Wells Housing Projects my whole life. If Dontae was anybody worth knowing I'd woulda knew him already. This meant he was a new player in the game. This could be possible, 'cause I'd been in the joint the last five years doing a dime for a manslaughter charge. While I was gone, a new breed of hustlers had jumped off the porch. But I was back to tell all their new asses that they needed to jump right back up on that muhfucka. While I was in, muhfuckas had been telling me the GDs had taken this bitch over. But I wasn't studdin' that shit, for real. I don't give a fuck about this new GD shit. As far as I'm concerned, joining a gang with the word gangster in it don't make you a gangster. You gotta be about that gangster shit to be a gangster. As for me, I'm a real gangster. I'm real fuckin' gangster. Ain't nothin' but blood and guts on my rap sheet. My shit is stamped.

I back peddled toward the rear exit of the building. "Y'all make sure y'all tell Dontae I said, if he got a problem with what I did here tonight, he can see me in the streets. My name's Reggie Wade and I ain't hard to find," I said, hikin' the trash bag further up on the shoulder. "Now," I continued. "I'ma count to three, and on three, I want all you muhfuckas to run out the front door. And don't stop runnin' til y'all get to King's Drive."

I glared around at the vics, they were shaking and shivering, and their teeth were chattering and shit. There was no way they were making it to King's Drive. But then again, them making it there wasn't more important than them running that way. I just needed them all running in a different direction than me.

11

I started counting, "One...two...thr..."

The vics took off all asses and elbows before I could finish my count. I almost laughed, fear is a muhfucka, it'll make a nigga hop a ten-foot wall. In no hurry at all, I did an about-face and walked out of the rear exit of the building. I had just killed a nigga in cold blood and signed my name in it. I don't run from static, I run to it. When my name is mentioned muhfuckas is petrified, that shit goes a long way in my line of work. A nigga don't mind losing his merch if he knows he can lose his life.

Straight like that.

CHAPTER 2
DONTAE

"Uh-uh, mister, I don't know where the hell you think you're goin'!"

I had thrown the heavy down comforter off my muscular, athletic frame when Princess came out of her sleep, turned over, and grabbed my arm. Princess is my bitch. She hates it when I leave her alone in our lakefront apartment. For a moment, I stood there and looked at her. She looks like Nia Long with longer hair, bigger lips, and a bad attitude. She's from Lawless Gardens, an apartment complex across the street from the Ida B. Wells Housing Projects, where I'm from. Lawless Gardens is nothin' but the projects minus the pissy hallways, the rundown buildings, and unemployed residents.

The people from there like to act like they're not from the projects. I met Princess in high school. That was before I dropped out. I took her to prom, took her virginity, and when we turned eighteen I took her with me to this plush apartment on the 11th floor of one of the flyest co-op buildings in Hyde Park. When I opened the windows in the summer I could hear the cold waters of Lake Michigan hit the sand. I could smell the water on the breeze. I could see the colorful sailboats disappearin' and reappearin' on the waves. The Ida B. Wells Housing Projects ain't far from here but it's far from here, you follow me?

"Princess," I said. "You know I gotta roll, bae. You always do this shit right before I leave."

She held onto my arm for dear life. "That's cause I don't want you to go," she whined. "Whenever you leave, you stay gone so long that I find myself wonderin' if somethin' happened to you."

"Stop thinkin' like that, bae. You stressin' yo' self out for no reason. I can't stay here with you all day. I gotta get out there and

13

get money. If I don't, who gon' pay the rent? Besides, don't you got classes to attend today?"

She let me go and crawled over to me. "Yeah, I gotta go to class, but that ain't for a couple more hours. We should be done by then."

"Done with what?" I asked her.

She looked at me with those hazel eyes. Her eyelids were heavy and her nipples were hard. I knew what she wanted. I just wanted to make her spell it out for me.

She grabbed my dick and squeezed it 'til it started gettin' hard. "Don't play with me, mister," she moaned in my ear. "You know what I want."

She started stroking me and looking into my eyes. "What you want me to do?" I loved it when she did that shit. "You want me to take it? You know I will if I have to."

I told her, "Take it then with yo' bad ass."

I don't know why I told Princess that cause as soon as I did, she pushed me down on the bed and put her hands, lips, and tongue to work on me. When she had worked up enough spit in her mouth, she licked around the head of my dick, up and down its shaft, then she slurped me in deep 'til I could feel the tight muscles of her throat massagin' my hardness. The slurpin' sounds she made as she sucked on me drove me insane. I loved the way she played with her nipples and her pussy to keep her free hand busy. I grabbed her head with both hands to show her my rhythm, stickin' that dick deep down in her throat 'til she choked and gagged. She almost had me about to nut when she spit me out and pulled her face back.

"Stop," she told me as she stroked my wet dick. "You messin' up my hair and shit. And why you tryna buss in my mouth, bae? You know where I want that shit."

"Where you want it, bae?" I asked her.

14

She didn't say nothing, she just got on the bed on all fours. Then she looked back at me, winked, and licked out her tongue. After that, she reached between her legs and pointed a French-Tip-nail at her well-manicured pussy. She had a pretty pussy, her lips were the same color as her skin. They gleamed with her juices, my body got hot.

She told me, "I want that shit right in here, bae. Put it right in here."

"I got you."

I put my tongue there first. I ate on her salty flesh 'til it oozed. Then I opened her soft ass cheeks and stuck my tongue in her booty, licking at her brown eye 'til she couldn't stand it. For a moment I went back and forth eating her pussy and eating her ass. The last time my tongue brushed over her clit her legs begin to tremble. She was cumming, I was always excited to make her cum.It made me feel good to make her feel good.

"Shit, bae!" she shouted.

I teased her as I fingered her wet pussy from behind. She grinded on my fingers and moaned.

"Who tryna buss in who mouth now?" I gloated.

"You lickin' my ass and shit," she moaned. "You know I can't take that."

Skillfully, I removed my fingers, and her juices dropped from them like water, as I grabbed her ass and slid my dick in her wet pussy from the back. I stroked her, goin' deep as I possibly could with every stroke. I slapped her ass, it jiggled. She threw that shit back at me. I pounded that pussy and she came, shaking and shivering. I stuck my thumb in her tight booty hole. She let a soprano note escape her lips. Then she put her face in the pillow and let it catch her screams. I reached around her and rubbed circles on her clit, never missin' a stroke. I beat her pussy up like a savage. In, out, in, out, round, and round. Now I had her waist, making her pussy meet my thrust.

Suddenly, I felt her pussy leaking and her walls grabbed my hard dick and started massaging it.

"Oohhh, bae," I groaned. "Do that shit. That shit feels good."
She got back to her hands. "You 'bouta nut?"
"Yeah...uh...huh."
"Stop, then. Lemme ride it."

I pulled out of her. My hard, veiny dick glistened with her juices. I grabbed it and stroked it. It throbbed like the beat of my heart as I got on my back and let Princess straddled me. She moved my hands and used her's to guide me inside her. Then she sat up, placed her palms on my chest, and started bouncin' her ass on me. I felt my dick head swell 'til it felt like it would bust. A tinglin' sensation rubbed me gently from head to toe.

"Here it comes too, bae," Princess said as she bounced on me faster. "Gimmie that nut. It's mine...it's mine...give it to me."

Suddenly, I felt like I got struck by lightin'. I came gruntin' and holdin' onto Princess ass cheeks tight. "Aahhh, shit," I mouthed out, breathlessly.

Princess kissed me. Then she dismounted like she was hoppin' off a horse, and laid down beside me. "That's your lil' boy right there, bae," Princess whispered in my ear.

"You think so?" I asked catching my breath.

"I know so."

Princess had been tryna get pregnant for the better part of a year. Even though she hadn't gotten a positive pregnancy test yet, that still hadn't stopped her from tryin'. The shit was all she could think about. As for me, I was content with waitin'. When it happened, it happened. That was all to it.

I crawled out of bed and left Princess dozin' off under the covers. In the bathroom mirror, I brushed my teeth and looked at the reflection starin' back at me. I was rockin' fresh cornrows. A fresh linin' framed my walnut complexion. The brown eyes, the wide nose, the lips, I could thank my father for all that. May he rest in peace.

I'm Dontae Devaughn Kirkpatrick. The only livin' son of Donavan *Baby Don* Kirkpatrick.

My daddy had been one of the realest dope dealers on the lower Southside of Chicago. That was before he was gunned down in a hail of bullets, right around the corner from where I live now. My daddy was a powerful man, but contrary to popular belief, I had not ridden his legacy to the top. I'd scratched, clawed, fought, and killed my own way to becomin' a boss in my own right. The twenty-three-year-old that looked back at me was official as a referee with a whistle.

Princess walked into the bathroom and turned on the shower. Then she slipped in, pulled the curtain back, and asked, "You gon' get in here with me. Or we doin' somethin' new now?"

We took showers together in the mornings.

I told her, "Nall, I'm gettin' in."

I stepped into the shower with her. The hot spray and the steam surrounded me, and my muscles relaxed.

Princess threw her arms around me and kissed me with so much tongue that I lost my breath. Then she sank to her knees and sucked me like a porn star. I fell back 'til I felt the cold tiles on my skin. My body tensed for a moment. I came in her mouth and she swallowed every drop.

She stood up. "I gotta keep them nuts empty, bae."

"Why?"

"Cause I don't want you fuckin' with none of them dirty ass project bitches," she said, smiling at me.

She always swore up and down I was fuckin' crazy bitches in the projects. I was. But she wasn't sure I was. That didn't stop her from fishin'.

I finished showerin' first. I heard the phone ringer when I walked out of the steamy bathroom with a colorful towel wrapped around my bottom half.

Riiinngggg! The phone was ringin' off the hook. I walked into the bedroom and answered the cordless, "What's up, Jo?"

"Folks, you need to get yo' ass down here," it was my nigga Cat Eyes. I could hear the distress in his voice. "You need to get down here to the building asap. On the real."

"What happened?"

"A muhfucka don' got all the way outta pocket, Folks. This shit nuts. You ain't gon' believe this."

"What is it, Jo?"

"I ain't gon' be reckless on the horn with you, Folks. Just get down here."

"A'ight, I'll be through there in a minute." I ended the call, wonderin' what had happened at the building. It was always some crazy shit goin' on. There is never a dull moment in *The Wells*.

I hopped into my underwear, black Guess jeans with the matchin' sweater, Bo Jackson's, and my black and white Pelle-Pelle leather. Then, I sat my Wing-Ding hat on my head and made for the door. Princess appeared in the doorway and blocked my exit. A white towel was wrapped around her head. The rest of her was still naked as the day she was born.

She asked me, "Where you off to so fast, mister?"

I told her, "I gotta be up. Cat Eyes just called me. I think some bullshit don' happened."

"I'm sick of him. Shoo...every time he calls you, you jump right up and run out the door like y'all fuckin, or somethin'," Princess said, disrespecting me and hoping I'd accept her invitation to the fight.

I just told her, "I gotta go, but remind me to check yo' ass later for that stupid shit that just flew outta yo' mouth." I walked out of the bedroom. I heard Princess talkin' shit behind me.

This is the Ida B. Wells Housing Projects. Four square miles of high-rises and low rises. The projects is broken up into six different areas. Each area has its own unique look. *The Zone* is the first area you see when you enter *The Wells* from King Drive. It's a maze of four-story low rises with front and back hallways.

Madden Park separates *The Zone* from *The Planet Rock* or *The Rock Block*, which resemble *The Zone*.

The only difference is there's some three-story low-rise and two-story bungalow-style rowhouses mixed into its maze. It's called *The Planet Rock* 'cause on 37th Place, there's a huge stone that blocks half the street. Back in the days, the huge stone used to be a flower bed, but now it was just grass and dirt and it had become a stash for the niggas that sell crack on the block. A little bit North and across 37th street is *The Extensions* which is a complex of seven-story buildings. Across Vincennes is an area known as *The BackYard* and a couple blocks South of *The BackYard* is *The Darrow Homes* a complex of orange fourteen-story buildings.

Across the street from the Darrow Homes is *The Madden Park Homes* which is called *Newtown* which is made up of six three-story low rises. The low-rises box in a basketball court and a grassy field like a prison yard, and three ten-story buildings stand around the low-rises like big brothers watchin' they little brother scrap. This is the Ida B. Wells Housing Projects. It's a concrete jungle, for real.

I bent a left at 37th and Vincennes and rode the 500 block West 'til I reached the 534 building. I'm from *The Extensions* area of the projects. *The Extensions* earned the nickname *The Body Bag Buildings* some years back 'cause for a while a body was bein' found every day.

I parked my black Benz 190 in the back parking lot. Then I hopped out and looked around. The first thing I noticed was that shop wasn't open. This wasn't like Cat Eyes and Fatso, two of my most trusted lieutenants. No matter what...the dope kept moving. Nothing stopped or interrupted our flow.

When my old man was killed, all he'd left my mother with was me and her dope habit. The day I turned thirteen, my mother came into my bedroom, handed me my old man's duffle bag, and said, "You need to go out there and get us some money. Your daddy's gone, but we still gotta eat. I know he taught you everythin' you need to know. Now, get out there and act like you got good sense."

I took the bag, and when I looked inside it, I found a hundred grams of China White Heroin, a Mr. Coffee grinder, a metal baker's sifter, some bottles of lactose, waxed playing cards, and a couple 1/8 spoons. I took my old man's old paraphernalia, bought some zip seals with bomb logos all over them, and turned that shit into *Bomb in a Bag* the most famous Heroin stamp on Chicago's gritty Southside. For over, a year now Bomb in a Bag been pumpin' $20 blows out of the 534 building. Fifty bags were inside of each bundle, which means each bundle was equivalent to $1,000 cash. I was currently moving twenty-five bundles a day. You do the math. That wasn't even counting the ends I made from niggas like Iroc Tony, Eddie Booze, and Jamo. They bought my bundles at a discount and sold them in other areas in the projects. I was making money hand over fist. That money was feeding a lotta niggas. That's why I had to find out what was going on.

"GD Folks," Cat Eyes said as he walked out of the rear exit of the building and came toward me. He was dressed for the breezy Fall day in a brown hoodie, a brown Coach bomber, jeans, and Gortex boots.

He'd been smoking weed already, which wasn't unusual cause he tended to smoke at least an ounce of weed a day. But as he got closer I could smell liquor on him, too. Cat Eyes didn't drink much alcohol, so I knew something was wrong. His green eyes looked grim. His light skin looked pale. His shoulders sagged like an old lady's titties.

I told him, "GD, Folks." I shook his hand with the Gangsters Disciple handshake. The shake was a simple palm slap and an entangling of the fingers that ended with a pitchfork. "What happened out here, Jo?"

"Some nigga named Reggie Wade came out here on the graveyard shift and stuck Folks nem up." Cat Eyes was salty. "He made Folks nem run out the building naked and ehthang, Gee. And that ain't all he did."

"Shit," I said, "That was enough to get his hat handed to him right there."

Cat Eyes nodded. "I know, Folks, but this shit gets worse."

"What can be worse than what he already did?" I asked him, wonderin' if the bad news could possibly get any worse.

"That nigga shot Fatso, Folks," Cat Eyes said, sadly. He seemed to be searching for a way to break some bad news to me.

"Did he kill him?" I asked, becoming impatient with his ass beating around the bush.

"He died in the hospital this morning."

From there I heard nothing else. Some nigga named Reggie Wade had stuck my spot up, killed my man, and sent my other niggas running naked in the streets. I had never felt so violated in my entire fuckin' life. Anger rose from my feet to my head, setting flame to my body, putting rocks in my jaws. I chewed on those rocks and clenched my fists, I could feel my nostrils flaring. Who the fuck is Reggie Wade? I took off walking toward the building.

"Folks, where you going?" Cat Eyes asked me.

"Grab shorty nem ass and get this shit back rollin'!" I shouted back at him. "I'ma take care of this other shit."

I walked into the building, bounded up the dark staircase 'til I reached the 5th floor. Then I ran down the hallway, to apartment 502, the crib I used as a momentary stash house. After keying myself in the crib, I walked in and grabbed my two.40 Glocks from under the refrigerator. I ended up back downstairs in the building lobby, where I ran back into Cat Eyes. This time he was with Sneak whose real name was Seneca but he hated that shit, so we never called him that. He was a slim nigga with a Bird's features and long shoulder-length cornrows that he wore parted down the middle and hanging to the side. While me, Fatso, and Cat Eyes had come up on the Monkey bars together, Sneak had moved to the building a few years ago from Stateway Gardens, but he was still one of the guys. Before he was working with us, the nigga was doing B & Es with a thieving ass nigga named Band-Aid. After Band-Aid had got himself killed breaking into a house in the suburbs one night, Sneak gave up on the thief shit.

Cat Eyes tapped Sneak's chest and told him, "Tell Folks what that bitch ass nigga said."

Sneak pulled a blunt out the pocket of his Taskforce pullover coat and fired up. "That nigga jumped yo' gate, Gee," Sneak said with smoke in his lungs. "He said if you had a problem with what he did you can see him in the streets, Gee. On the Boss."

Whenever a GD said, *"On the Boss."* He was hangin' the truth on the name of Larry Hoover, the undisputed king of the Gangster Disciples. Most niggas was lying when they used Larry's name, but not my niggas. Sneak continued, "Then that nigga had the nerve to drop his government, Gee. His bitch ass got cast iron nuts. If I catch him I'ma set his ass on fire with that choppa."

"You ain't gon' do shit, Sneak," I told him. "You gon' fall back."

I looked at Cat Eyes. "You too, Jo. This my static right here. A nigga gotta answer to me for this ho' ass shit." I walked out of the building, headed across the fire lane to the 510 building. I didn't know who Reggie Wade was, but I knew who did.

CHAPTER 3
PRINCESS

I'm one of them pretty bitches. I keep my hair whipped, my mani-Pedi stay on some fresh shit, my hazel eyes are pretty, my honey-colored skin is pretty, my flat stomach is pretty. Told you, I'm one of them pretty bitches. I'm one of them fly bitches. Gucci, Louis, Chanel, Fendi are my shit, all my shit, I don't fuck with it if it ain't made by the top designers. Diamonds are definitely this girl's best friend. I drive a brand-new red BMW. My man bought me that shit for my birthday. Said he saw it and he just knew it was for me 'cause it was fly. I ain't a dumb bitch either. I'm in my second year of college at Chicago State University and in two more years, I'll have my Bachelor's in Finance Administration.

After that, I already got a job lined up with a bank downtown. Now that I don' told y'all a little about me, I bet y'all already about to ask me, if you got all this shit goin' for yourself. Why are you fuckin' with a dope dealin', gangster, like Dontae? The answer is simple, he loves me, he protects me, and he takes real good care of me. I can't front that nigga gives me that good ass mornin' sex. He eats this pussy from the back and sticks his tongue in my booty. Then he gives me that big nine-inch pipe 'til I come three times. My bae gives it up like that on the regular and I'm satisfied. That's enough about me right now 'cause that ain't even the vibe I'm on this morning.

My friend Angie called me a little while ago and told me a nigga killed her baby's daddy. Which explained why Dontae had left the house in such a rush. I fucks with Angie. We been tight since elementary school. So, I had to take a day off from my classes to comfort her durin' her loss. God forbid something like this ever happened to Dontae. I don't think I'd know what to do.

Traffic was a muhfucka, the sun was hidin' behind the clouds and the wind was blowing hard enough to blow away a small kid when I pulled up in to the Lakegrove complex. Angie's complex reminded me of my own Lawless Gardens. The only difference was Lakegrove's buildings were white, and they were on 35th and Cottage Grove.

I parked beside a silver Ford Taurus. I hated the Taurus. My first car had been a Ford Tempo, and it had broken down on me at least once a month. I crawled out of my Beamer, walked across the parkin' lot like it was a NY runway. I was rocking a black Chanel jumpsuit, ankle-high black Chanel boots, and the matching Chanel bag. In my ears were these cold, ass Chanel Bangles, and my hair was laid on my head in a neat wrap. I couldn't help it. I knew this was a sad occasion, but I saw no reason for me to forego being fly.

I walked through the glass doors, buzzed Angie's apartment and she instantly buzzed me in. I was here to comfort and console my friend, but I hoped she didn't get her tears all over my Chanel jumpsuit. When tears dried on this fine-cut silk they wrinkled it. I was too fly of a bitch to be walking around with wrinkles.

Upstairs, I walked into Angie's apartment and found her a mess. She had on a t-shirt and sweats. Her hair was in a messy bun. Her eyes were red and puffy and she was rockin' her three-year-old son Rashaun on the sofa. Rashaun was a cute little brown boy, but this shit wasn't cute.

She cried, "He's dead, Princess. Fatso is dead."

My girl was broken up. I didn't know what to say. I just looked at her with tears wellin' up in my eyes. Angie was a little thing. But somehow Fatso's death had made her even smaller as a friend. I needed to do something to comfort her in her time of grief. I unbuckled my Chanel boots. I had to kick them bitches off 'cause even though they were fly, they were starting to hurt my feet. I reached my arms out to her.

I told her, "Gimme Rashaun."

She handed her little boy over to me. His little tear-stained face was asleep. I took him in my arms, walked with him into his bedroom, and tucked him under his Disney sheets. Then I left his bedroom, walked to my girl's peninsula kitchen, and went into her cabinet where I found a bottle of Hen. After grabbin' two glasses out of the top utensil holder on the granite countertop, I walked back into the living room.

"I got just what you need, bitch," I said as I sat down and poured us up. I knew the Hen wouldn't be enough, so I went into my purse, pulled out the weed I'd stolen from Dontae's stash, and rolled up.

"You know I don't smoke," Angie said.

I fired up a joint, hit it, then handed it to her and told her, "You gon' smoke some today. Cause I'll be damn if I have you fallin' apart on me in here. We some strong bitches. You gotta be strong, bitch."

"That's easy for you to say," Angie told me as she hit the joint. "Dontae ain't dead."

I had no response. Angie was right. I'd probably be broken up right now if it was Dontae who had been killed. Being the girlfriend of a street nigga meant you lived under the threat of knowing you could lose your man at any moment. The shit was super stressful. That's why I never liked Dontae being away from me too long. If anything ever happened to him I wouldn't know what to do.

"Do you know what happened?" I asked Angie as we smoked and drank.

She wiped her tears away with the tail of her t-shirt and said, "All I know is there was a robbery in the building, and the robber shot Fatso. His momma been in touch with the police, but you know they don't be investigatin' drug-related murders like that. They gon' let whoever did this get away with it, for real, for real."

I felt sorry for Angie, and I'm almost sure that showed on my face. I told her, "Whoever did this to Fatso won't get away with it."

Angie put her joint out, took a sip from her Hen, and asked me, "How can you be so sure about that, Princess?"

I told her flat out, "You know them GD niggas over there is off the chain. And Dontae, Cat Eyes, and Sneak are the worse ones. They gon' catch that nigga that killed Fatso. And when they do, he gon' wish he went to jail for what he did."

I sat there with Angie for the rest of the day, drinkin' and smokin' and helpin' her numb her pain. Long periods of silence fell between us, and there were times that I knew she was thinkin' about how she'd get through the loss of her baby's daddy. My thoughts were about Dontae and what this meant for him. He was the vengeful type. He never let things go. He would never rest 'til Fatso's killer was dead. A look of worry crossed my face. Fatso's death meant war for Dontae. The problem is, in war, no one is a winner. I wondered if Dontae understood this.

CHAPTER 4
DONTAE

"Pool Hall, who the fuck is Reggie Wade?"

A nigga done came through my dope line, tore me off for some ends, and killed my man Fatso. I run a $100,000 a week business. Clockin' them kinda gees makes it possible for me to put some bread on a nigga's head, but I can't do that. That shit would make me look weak, and I can't afford to look weak out here in these streets. Niggas smell weakness from miles away and exploit that shit. This is my business to handle. my static. The nigga Reggie Wade had called me out. I'm taking that shit personally. Plus, I ain't into payin' a nigga to do no dirt for me that I can do for myself. Furthermore, this is a straight-up violation. If I allow this shit to slide, every nigga with a gun will be lined up tryna get a piece of my ass. Never that move, I must retaliate. There is no way I can allow this violation to go unanswered. If I let this ride, it would go against everything I stand for and make me feel lesser than a man.

But first thing first, I had to know what I was up against. That's why I was at Pool Hall's cramped apartment tryna to pry information out of him. Pool Hall was one of the junkies that ran customers off 39th Street to my spot. He had a knack for detecting good dope and a slick tongue. He'd been one of the biggest dope dealers in the city back in the day, but the sea of the game had long swallowed him up and spit him back out on the shore. His hair looked like old steel, wool, his face was scarred like a fighting pitbull and what was left of his teeth was grayish-brown and leaning like headstones in an old cemetery.

An oversized dingy Salem cigarette t-shirt swallowed his scrawny frame, and the green polyester slacks hangin' off his ass looked like he'd closed his eyes, dug to the bottom of a box at the

27

Salvation Army, pulled them out, and jumped his ass right into them muhfuckas. Pool Hall had once been king but now he was only a peasant. Still, I knew he was a griot of the game in these projects. If anybody knew Reggie Wade I knew it would be him. Pool Hall reached up and scratched at his scruffy beard. The shit sounded like matches being struck. He looked at me with sleep in his eyes.

"Bossman, what you doin' here? It's early as Moe, Larry, and Curly. What time is it?" he asked me as he used a big knuckle to wipe away the crust in his eyes.

I checked my Movado. "It's time for you to get yo old ass up."

"Old?" he said, jerking his body like he was offended. "You better hope you get my age, you young street punk. I know I ain't in the best shape, but neither is the marathon runner when he comes..." He leaned forward a little. "...bustin' through that finish line."

"I hear you."

"I know it, bossman. You too near me not to hear me."

I laughed. "You gon' let me in? Or we gon' stand here talkin' shit all day, old nigga?"

He turned and walked away from the door. "My bad, bossman," he apologized. "Come right on in and lock her up behind you. Me casa is su casa."

I locked up and followed Pool Hall through the hallway. His bare feet sounded like skis slidin' across hard snow. The smell of weeks-old ass and stale cigarettes slapped me in the face.

I gagged.

"I kinda figured I might get a visit from you this mornin'," he said as he shuffled into his bedroom. "Have a seat, bossman, I'll be out in a sec."

I walked into the living room and looked around. The yellow film on the walls was thick as butter. I got the impression that if I rubbed up against them, they would stain my clothes. Pool Hall had furnished his crib like an old mechanic garage. A busted, bucket seat and a tattered brown sofa were situated around a table made out of a couple of milk crates and a slab of plywood, scattered all over the plywood surface was hypodermic needles, burned bottlecaps, broken cigarette lighters, and cotton balls. A soft pack of Salem 100s sat crumpled beside a dinted tin ashtray. The mornin' sun spilled in through the grimy living room window and dust danced around in beams of sunlight. I wanted to sit down, so I glanced at the bucket seat and decided to take my chances with the bucket seat and sat down. Pool Hall shuffled out of his bedroom. His feet were now stuffed into an old pair of black wing tips that he'd cut the back out of and made into slippers.

He took a seat on the sofa and fell further into it than he liked. So, he sat up, grabbed his cigarettes, and fired up.

"Pool Hall," I said. "Who the fuck is Reggie Wade?"

A cough escaped the old man that sounded like a muffler backfirin'.

Then he said, "It's been a lil' while since I heard that name."

"So, you know him, huh?" I asked him.

He looked at me like we were the last two players in a poker hand. We were all in, but he had a better hand than me.

"I'm sick as a dog, bossman," he said, shootin' me his spiel. "You gotta wake up for me? You know I need my wake up."

Luckily, I had anticipated Pool Hall's move. I knew there was no way he was talkin' to me without havin' his mornin' shot of dope. So, I reached into the inside pocket of my Pelle-Pelle, fished out a bag of dope, and tossed it onto the plywood table. Pool Hall club fingers and curved fingernails shot out like a grapplin' hook. He snatched up the baggie of dope, sat his cigarette in the ashtray, and started preparin' his shot.

Impatience moved me around on the bucket seat. "Come on, Pool Hall. That nigga robbed and killed Fatso. I ain't got all day. Do you know the nigga or not?"

Pool Hall moved his hand as if to tell me to pump my brakes. "Be easy, bossman. You know I can hardly think straight without my medicine. Hold on a minute and lemme get my medicine in me. Then, we gon' rap, Jack. You pickin' up what I'm puttin' down?"

I curled my top lip and took a deep breath. "Hurry up, old ass nigga..."

I hated patience. It was somethin' I seriously needed to work on. Shit was transactional with me. If I paid you, I expected you to move when I said move. Pool Hall hadn't got that memo. Any other time I would've been up and out of here. But not today, I needed information.

So, I sat there while Pool Hall emptied a sixth of Heroin into a beer bottle cap, where he added a couple of drops of lemon juice, then held a cigarette lighter under it 'til it sizzled. After that, he dropped a tiny piece of the cotton ball onto the now liquified Heroin and stuck his syringe into the cotton ball. I saw him trembling as he drew the dope up into the vial of his syringe. Suddenly, I heard a sound that reminded me of an 8-ball break. After that, I smelled some shit that stank like the ass of a garbage truck. I balled my face up and pinched my nostrils closed.

"Gotdamn old ass nigga! What the fuck was that stankin' ass shit?" I shouted.

Pool Hall tapped the vial of his syringe. Then he looked at me and said, "Oh...my bad, bossman. That was me, I fart before I shoot dope. It usually ain't foul," he said, pausin' to sniff the air. "I ate some cold pork and beans last night, and that shit didn't agree with my stomach."

I shook my head, then I got up and opened a window. When I sat down again, Pool Hall was usin' his belt to find a vein. He had the belt around his arm like a hangman's noose.

He stuck the tail of it between what was left of his rotten teeth and said, "That was Fatso who got killed over there last night, huh?"

I told him, "Yeah, that nigga Reggie Wade shot folks in the chest with a gauge."

I had been in the dope game since I was thirteen, but my stomach still did somersaults when I saw Pool Hall's arms and hands. His arms looked like ham hocks with a squiggly mess of broken veins, tracks, and abscesses. That shit bled and pussed if he stretched too far. His hands were even more disgustin' they looked like rubber gloves with air in 'em and the skin on his back hands could've been the bottom of a tin ashtray. The shit made me sick to my stomach. I almost hurled right there on the floor. Though I had been thoroughly disgusted already, I sat there and waited for Pool Hall to finish shootin' his dope. He pushed the dope into his vein. I saw his eyes flutter, his body sagged, and the dope mask came down on his mug like a window shade. He nodded a bit. Then he pulled the needle out of his arm, sat it on the table, and took his belt off his arm.

"So, they don' let that fool, Reggie Wade, out huh, bossman?" Pool Hall said, soundin' like a frog.

"I need to know everything you know about the nigga, Pool Hall. His ass bogus for the shit he pulled. And I'm 'bouta put some straightener on that shit."

Pool Hall scratched at his dope itch. Dope fiends always scratched when the dope was good.

"I know all them Wades," Pool Hall said.

In the projects, if people knew you by your family name you had a big family. The only other thing besides death and poverty here was family heritage. "I know the whole damn family, from the grandma down. They all crazy as bessy bugs. Reggie Wade's momma was Cynthia Wade. Everybody called her Cynt. Lil' tough bitch that used to run around the projects slashin' bitches with boxcutters and shit. A nigga named Buster Stevens turned her out on the horse and had her sellin' pussy, but she slowed down when she started havin' them, babies."

"How many did she have?" I asked.

31

Pool Hall's cigarette had burned out in the ashtray, so he fired up another. "The bitch had three babies," he said. "And she shot dope all the way through every last pregnancy."

"No wonder that nigga a dope fiend," I commented. "That's cold."

"You think that's cold, huh?" Pool Hall said. "Lil' bitch was in Crutcher's shootin' gallery when her water broke for the third time. The spike was still in her arm when the ambulance came."

Pool Hall's story about Reggie Wade's mother usin' drugs while she was pregnant didn't surprise me, but you would think a pregnant woman would have enough respect for her unborn child's life to stop usin' and abusin' while she was pregnant. You would think, but I had come to expect a drug addict not to respect someone else's life. How could a drug addict respect someone else's life when they couldn't respect their own?

I looked at Pool Hall, and his old ass just kept on scratchin'. That shit made my skin crawl.

I never understood the whole dope-itch thing. But then again, I didn't want to understand. Everything ain't for everybody.

I asked him, "Where his momma at now?"

I figured if I could find Reggie Wade's mother I could find him. Even the worst nigga stopped by to visit momma every now and again.

"She's dead as a do' knob, bossman. Got a hold of some bad shit a few years back and checked out of this roach motel we call life. A housin' worker found her stankin' and stiff as a board in a vacant apartment over there in the rowhouses," he said this, then smashed out his cigarette in the ashtray.

I felt a spring sticking me in my ass. Shit hurt like a bitch, I adjusted myself on the bucket seat.

"What was she doin' in there?" I asked.

Pool Hall nodded and scratched a bit and told me, "Bitch probably was hidin', tryna be greedy with her shit. Fuck around and went out and wasn't nobody 'round to help her ass. When they found her, the rats had ate half her face off." He frowned and shook his head. "Sad state of affairs."

Yeah, it was a sad state of affairs but not 'cause Cynt had overdosed in a vaco and had half her face eaten off by rats. It was a sad state of affairs for me 'cause with Reggie Wade's mother dead, I knew it would be that much harder to find him. I was stuck for a moment. Then, all of a sudden, I remembered that Pool Hall had told me Cynt had three kids.

I asked Pool Hall, "What's up with Cynt's other two kids?"

Pool Hall fired up again and told me, "Rachel's the oldest, then Ronnie. And both of them mo' fucked up in the head than Reggie is. His sister Rachel killed that nigga Buster Steven when she was 'bout fourteen."

"Straight up?" I asked with surprise in my voice. "Why she do the nigga?"

"The creep ass nigga had been roughin' the lil' girl off since she was old enough to start school. She fixed his ass, though. Caught him sleep and sat in his chest with a butcher knife. Stabbed him thirty-six times."

My eyelids and eyebrows shot up. "She butchered his ass, Jo'," I said.

"She shole did," Pool Hall replied. "But that ain't all. She cut the nigga's dick off down to the balls and stuck that shit in his mouth. When them people asked her why she did it, she told 'em the nigga had been forcin' her to suck his dick since she was seven."

I shook my head.

Pool Hall continued, "Them folks said she was nuts and they sent her ass straight to Tinley Park. Don't pass go, don't collect two hunnid' dollars."

Tinley Park was an insane asylum out in the southern suburbs of Cook County. The place was reserved for the craziest the city had to offer.

"So, you ain't heard nothin' else about her since the murder?" I asked.

He shook his head. "Nope, bossman, but I 'spect' she in a padded room somewhere pullin' her hair out her head."

Pool Hall chain-smoked till I knew the smell of Salem cigarettes would be in my clothes, and the air was damn near unbreathable. I wanted to leave, but I had to drain him of as much information as I could. The more information I had about Reggie Wade, the more likely I was to catch him and buss his shit.

Pool Hall went on, "Reggie Wade's brother Ronnie was The Front Door Rapist. He would rape a bitch, slit her throat, then lean her on her apartment door and knock 'til someone came to the door. If someone answered the door, the body would fall into the apartment, and a scream would follow, that muhfuckas only heard in horror flicks. This was the old Ida B. Wells. Back when burnin' mattresses, vacuum cleaners, and car tires used to come flyin' out of seven-story windows and fall on your head if you wasn't careful. Ronnie got caught back then. He's servin' a natural life sentence. I told you they's all crazy as bessy bugs," Pool Hall said.

"Crazy ain't the word."

I sat there lettin' everything Pool Hall told me settle in on me like fog on a misty night. Reggie Wade's mother, a whore and a stomp-down dope fiend, his sister a victim of childhood molestation, a killer of her childhood molester, his brother a serial rapist, and a killer. I couldn't help but admit the obvious. Reggie Wade had a helluva pedigree. Made me not even want to hear Reggie Wade's story. However, I knew I needed to. Only a fool played a game without knowin' the rules.

I looked at Pool Hall and he'd fallen into a deep nod. His mouth was open. His tongue was hanging and he was slobbering. He looked like a bulldog. He swayed in his seat till I thought he would fall over. Just before he did, he caught himself and started swaying again. He did all of this as he scratched his nuts like that bulldog had fleas. He was high as a Boeing 747.

"Pool Hall!" I shouted.

He came out of his nod, running a pasty tongue around his mouth and over his chapped lips. Then, he reached up and used his club fingers to wipe away the white in the corners of his lips.

I told him, "Pool Hall, stay with me old nigga."

He said, "That shit you gave me don' jumped off the top turn buckle and hit me with a cold-blooded elbow, bossman. You outdid yo' self with this one. But where was I?"

I sat back on the bucket seat. "Reggie Wade," I reminded him.

"Oh, yeah, Reggie Wade," Pool Hall said this, fired up another cigarette, and continued, "By the time Cynt had Reggie Wade, she wasn't even fakin' like she was tryna raise another kid. Plus, I think that boy was kinda slow. He ain't say a word till he was 'bout seven years old. He was just as weird. Used to be round here killin' strays and shit, you know? Like one of them psycho sociopath muhfuckas."

I listened as Pool Hall went on tellin' me Reggie Wade's life story, or rather what he knew of it. He told me the nigga dropped out early and went to snatchin' purses and stealin' and shit. He told me he had a friend named Cornbread that was found in the basement on a rowhouse building with a bullet in his head. The boy was holdin' on to a .38 special. The police had ruled the death a suicide, but a resident in the building had seen Reggie Wade creep out of the basement that night.

I was surprised.

"The twist ain't pick him up?"

Pool Hall nodded. "Yeah, they picked him up. But the boy ain't say shit. I mean not a word. They had him evaluated by the head doctors, but nothin' else came of it. He was only thirteen."

I shook my head.

"That nigga ain't ever been no good."

Pool Hall shook his head.

"The same shit happened again a few years later," Pool Hall said as he sat back and crossed his right leg over his left. "Had everybody scratchin' their head 'round here. Why everybody 'round Reggie Wade so depressed and suicidal? It came out later that the boy was takin' money and don't like to share his stains. If he takes somthin' with a joker, he ain't got no intention on playin' palms up. It's all about playin' for keeps with him. He got worse when he started gettin' high."

Pool Hall told me Heroin for Reggie Wade was an acquired taste. He inherited the addiction from his mother. When he got strung out, he got thirsty, robbing everything moving.

I knew the effects of Heroin. How addictive it was, how necessary it was to addicts, how hard it was to kick. Bein' dope sick would make a coldblooded coward rob the police in front of the station in broad daylight. A junkie was different than a crackhead. If you sat somethin' valuable down in front of a crackhead, when you turned yo' head it'd be gone. But when you were fucking with a junkie you didn't have to turn your head for your shit to be gone. A junkie would take it.

"He robbed Iroc Tony," Pool Hall said. "But Iroc Tony caught up with his ass a week later and put him on an iron diet."

Pool Hall said this and smashed another cigarette out in the ashtray. "That was right before the nigga caught his bid."

I knew Iroc Tony. He was one of the GD Folks that bought my bundles wholesale and sold 'em in Newtown, the area he was from. Iroc Tony was a nigga that never really played with them pistols. He only popped his thang if he had to. I was sure that Reggie Wade had violated him in some kind of way to make him get on that.

"But now Iroc Tony gotta be on his P's and Q's cause the boy don't forget or forgive shit. That's one thing about him, bossman, he all about the even-steven. If you plan on goin' at him, I highly suggest you get close enough to him to smell his breath and knock his noodles out. Don't play with him, 'cause like I told you. He plays for keeps."

Without realizing it, my eyebrows had met in the middle of my head, my forehead was pleated like a pair of old slacks, and my top lip was curled back enough to show some of my top row. Also, my hands had found their way into the pockets of my jacket. Where they wrapped themselves around my twin .40s. All that was on my mind was walkin' that nigga Reggie Wade down and bussing his shit.

Pool Hall described him, tall, lanky, dark as an eclipse. He wore a perm pulled back into a ponytail, and he wore a black trench coat and Hi-Tec boots. He told me the nigga might have a slight limp and he walked with his ass stuck out like a bitch.

I asked Pool Hall, "What's that all about?"

Pool Hall became serious, "Buster Stevens was a freak ass muhfucka, bossman. He might've been fuckin Reggie, too."

Sickened by what Pool Hall had just said, I cringed. I figured what he said about Reggie Wade might be true. But hearin' that shit was still disgustin'. I sat up and switched the subject. "You know where I can find the nigga?"

"You find him where you find all the other low down dirty muhfuckas." Pool Hall spat as he shrugged his bony shoulders. "In the gutter with the rest the bowling pins. Holla at that lil' punk bitch Streetlight. She probably can point you in the right direction."

Streetlight, I knew who she was, but I didn't know her. She was Grace Jones, heavier on the top and bottom. Her name wasn't Streetlight, but she got her money turning tricks at the streetlights up on 39th Street. A rumor was going around about her having that package. However, the streets always talked that way about mud kickers. So, I didn't know how true that talk was. It didn't matter to me either way. I wasn't tryna fuck her raw. I just needed to ask her a few questions. That's all.

Armed with enough intel, and with ice runnin' through my veins, I got on my feet and readied myself for my mission. I had to find Reggie Wade and kill his ass in Chicago gangland slaying fashion. The level of disrespect he had perpetrated against me was off the meter. The nigga had forced my hand.

"I'm outta here, old nigga," I told Pool Hall. "Thanks for the help."

Pool Hall threw a fat hand at me. "Somethin' small to a giant," he told me. "You know Fatso was my man. You just remember what I told you, bossman. Get close enough to him to smell his breath. Don't play with the nigga, 'cause..."

"He plays for keeps," I said, finishing his thought. "He ain't the only one."

I turned and made for the door, but by the time I reached the hallway.

Pool Hall called me, "Bossman?"

I turned to face him. "What up?"

He cocked his head to the side and gave me puppy eyes. "You got some more dope on you?"

I shook my head. "I'll tell Cat Eyes to look out for you," I told him.

"Right on, bossman," Pool Hall told me raisin' a fat fist.

I walked out of Pool Hall's crib, hands on my .40s, fingers on the trigger. "Where you at Reggie Wade? Let's do this shit and get it over with."

CHAPTER 5
REGGIE WADE

"Oh, shit...oh...shit! That's right, baby. Fuck me!"

I was fuckin' the cowboy shit out of Mi-Mi my lil' primo smokin' bitch from the 520 building. I had a yard of dick in her from the back, stabbin' her pussy relentlessly, as she screamed like a rape victim.

"Awww! I can...feel...this dick...in my stomach!"

"Shut up and take this dick, vic," I told her as I stroked her and slapped her ass.

I had been fucking Mi-Mi since I'd been back in the world. I couldn't even lie, I was getting a little attached to her punk ass. I wasn't even tripping about her not being the baddest bitch. Her skin was a little bad and she had a gap in her teeth. But she had a bomb on the head and she kept that pussy shaved nice and clean, which was more than I could say for the rest of these hoes around the projects. On top of that, me and Mi-Mi had history. She was one of my pieces before I did my bid, so she knew my life, and I didn't have to train her. As long as I had a couple of bags of crack for her when I came in at night, I didn't have to hear her mouth. Off a couple of primo joints, the bitch would fuck and suck all night long, and that's all I could ask for after a long night of robbin' and killin'.

"Ooh, baby," Mi-Mi moaned as she turned her big juicy ass in a circle on this dick.

"Trust and believe...I'm 'bout to cum all on this...oooh...dick!"

I clawed at her ass 'til I had handfuls of dimpled ass cheeks. Then I started bringin' her pussy back to meet my every stroke. She took my thrusts like a big girl.

"Shit, baby!" Mi-Mi screamed as she played in her pussy. "This pussy 'bouta...it's bouta...aah!"

I felt her pussy muscles contractin' on me as she trembled and came in ocean waves. I sped up my stokes and fucked her through her orgasm. That pussy got wetter, and her juices squirted all over my stomach. I could feel that shit leakin' all over my balls. Her increasin' wetness made her pussy feel like a wet tight glove stroking my hard dick. That feeling and her moans were about to take me there.

"I feel that dick in me gettin' harder, baby," Mi-Mi moaned as she threw her ass back on me. "Don't pull out this time. Buss that nut in this pussy." She looked back at me with her tongue out. "That's it, baby buss that nut in this wet ass pussy. You gon' do that for me?"

"Hell muthafuckin' yeah!" I groaned as I stroked her faster and deeper.

Suddenly, I felt the head of my dick tingling. I closed my eyes, concentrated on my nut, came all inside Mi-Mi's wet pussy, and collapsed beside her.

She slithered down my body, stroked my sticky dick, and looked up at me. "You're an animal, baby," Mi-Mi said, smiling freakily at me. "When you get that dope in you, you be all up in this pussy like it's yours."

"It is mine?" I asked her. "Right?"

"Nall," she checked me, "it's mine," she said, then reached in her pussy and sucked her fingers as she stroked me. "And this pussy good, too. Ain't it, baby?"

"Best I ever had," I said smiling. I almost meant it, but there was a pussy I'd had that was better...at least one.

She stopped stroking me and gave me a dry-ass look. "You so full of shit it's pathetic, baby. But I still fuck with yo' black ass."

"How I'm full of shit? When I just asked you if that pussy was mine and you told me no?"

Mi-Mi started stroking my dick again. "I'll tell you what," she said in between licks around the head of my dick. "We can share this pussy. I can't just give her to you." She reached in her pussy again and stuck her fingers in her mouth. "She tastes too good." She held her fingers out to me. "Want some?"

I told her, "Yeah, gimme some."

She reached up and I sat up then tasted her fingers. They tasted sweet and salty.

Mi-Mi was a freak, she had turned me out since I'd been back on this side of the wall and I loved that shit.

I told her, "Why don't you gon' head play that horn for me?"

She licked my dick and it snapped back to attention. "What song you want me to play?"

I told her to play *Between The Sheets* by *The Isley Brothers*. After I told her that, she spit on my dick and stuck it into her mouth. When it reached her throat, she began humming the old school groove. The stimulation moved through my body like an electric current. I closed my eyes and relaxed as she sucked me dry. My nut came faster than I wanted it to. Mi-Mi got out of bed and left the room as if she had conquered me, on some drop the mic shit.

Now that my tension was released, I crawled out of bed and walked over to Mi-Mi's closet. The Beast leaned on the back of it, behind her shoes, along with the trash bag of merch I'd taken last night. I stood there gazing at The Beast and the trash bag. It was full of dope bundles, crack, jewelry, and some other shit. Altogether I had stained them pussy ass niggas for over $6,000 and to think, all I had to do was kill a nigga for it. That was light work.

I reached into the bag and retrieved some rocks and blows. Then, I walked over to Mi-Mi's dresser. It was an old wooden piece of shit. One of those pieces you see in a secondhand store. Yet, its surface was smooth. So, I laid out a bag of dope and rolled a primo joint.

As I snorted the dope and rolled the primo, I heard the toilet flush, then I heard the shower. Mi-Mi had taken a shit. She always took a shower after she shitted. She was clean. I loved a clean ass bitch. The quickest way for a bitch to get killed fuckin' with me, was for her to have cottage cheese in her panties and crust in her ass.

Mi-Mi sashayed back into the bedroom. Her cinnamon skin was moist from her shower. Her nipples looked like Hershey's kisses, and the lips of her fleshly pussy were blowing me a kiss through the curls between her thighs. I thought about prison for a moment. I thought about the nights I looked at hardcore porn magazines like Black Tails and Video illustrated and jagged my dick off 'til it was raw. As I dreamed about being in the same room with a bitch with some good pussy.

I didn't have to dream anymore.

"Here, Vic," I said handing Mi-Mi the primo joint I rolled for her. "Hit that."

She took it from me and hit it 'til the crack sizzled on the weed. The gaze in her eyes told me she was high out of her mind. She took the joint over to the bed.

I stood there and finished off the dope on the dresser. Then I held my head back and closed my eyes as I waited for the dope to drain.

Afterward, I thought about the murder I'd committed in the 534 building. I thought about fat boy words, they echoed off the empty hall of my mind, *"I'm just sayin...Dontae gon' be on yo' ass about his shit."* The threat in the fat boy's words was evident but that shit didn't spook me. I don't spook easy. However, what didn't sit right with me was how sure fat boy was about what he'd said. The problem was I didn't know Dontae from a hole in the ground. In this business, you had to be able to put names with faces. Not having a name to go with a face could get your shit split. That's why I had always made it my business to know all the players in the game. If for no other reason but for seeing the trap before I fell into it. As much as I believed I was the hunter and never the prey, I knew the streets. In the streets, it was law, that there wasn't a nigga alive that couldn't be touched. I had fucked up. I had made my first major mistake since I'd been home. I had robbed a faceless name. *Who the fuck is Dontae and why was fat boy so sure he'd be on my ass?*

"Baby?" Mi-Mi whined.

"What's up, Vic?" I replied coming out my thoughts.

My eyes shot over to the bed. Mi-Mi was lying there with her back on the headboard, joint between her lips, gray and blue clouds of fragrant smoke billowing and hallowing around her head. The thick braids she was wearing had her looking like a Rasta.

She opened her legs and rubbed circles around her clit. "You gon' gimme some more of that dope dick, or what?"

"I got yo' frantic ass, Vic," I told her as I grabbed my dick and walked it over to her.

When I crawled onto the bed and mounted Mi-Mi, she spread her legs under and took every inch of me with ease. I felt her fingernails in my back as I pounded away at the pussy, and as I fucked her all I could think about was Dontae and the words fat boy had said before I sent him to whatever afterlife awaited him. Suddenly, I knew I wouldn't rest easy without knowing who Dontae was. I had to put a face with the name. This was the only way to keep the cheat off me. As for right now, I felt more like the prey than the hunter. I had to change that shit, fast.

"I'm just sayin...Dontae gon' be on yo' ass about this shit." Fat boy's words replayed in my head.

Not if I get on his ass first.

CHAPTER 6
CAT EYES

"Bomb in a Bag! Bomb in a Bag! Bomb in a Bag!" I shouted at the cars pulling up in the front parking lot of the 534 building. Dope fiends bailed out of cars and formed a line that snaked around the building, up to its front door. "Stay in line, y'all. Don't worry about this good dope runnin' out. We got enough for everybody," I said and the dope fiends obeyed my order.

They didn't have a choice. I ran the day-to-day operation of Bomb in a Bag. Fatso was the one that really ran the line. But now he was gone, so I had to step up and keep this shit goin'. The game don't stop when one player gets popped. The Folks out here still had to eat.

"Bomb in a Bag! Bomb in a Bag! Bomb in a Bag!"

The lunch rush was in full swing and this shit was rolling. A nigga ain't seen shit 'til he sees thousands of people converging on one particular place to cop dope in broad daylight. I'm telling you it's a sight to behold.

"Aye, Cat Eyes, c'mere!"

I heard my name called and looked toward 37th Street. I was standing in the eye of a dope fiend storm when I saw Princess sittin' in her shiny, red Beamer, hair and nails were perfect, honey brown skin glowing, beautiful full lips glossy, diamonds and gold flicking in the October sun. Princess had the prettiest hazel eyes that I'd ever seen. Her curves were on some model shit. She was sexy as a muhfucka, even her feet were pretty. Dontae definitely had a bad bitch. But that bitch wasn't shit. For starts the bitch was a freak.

44

I could see it in her eyes, I knew those eyes. I had those eyes and I was a freak. So, that's how I knew she was a freak, too. Another way I could tell she was a freak was by the way she looks at me whenever Dontae wasn't around. Another nigga's bitch don't' look down between another nigga's legs, then look back up in his eyes 'less that bitch was tryna fuck. When I was in the county jail I met a nigga named Ju-Ju from the Ickies Housing Projects. He told me he had fucked Princess and she sucked his dick.

The nigga wasn't lying either, 'cause he knew about the rose and thorns tattoo on her thigh. I believed Ju-Ju, so when I got out of the county I told Dontae about Ju-Ju and what he told me. Dontae didn't believe the nigga's story. Said that nigga was jealous and just pouring salt 'cause he wanted Princess. After that, all I could do was shake my head and walk away. That bitch Princess had my nigga Dontae's nose wide open. It was sickening to see.

I mean, look at the bitch? The chain she got on is nasty and 14 karat gold. The diamond on her finger is Marquis and I know it's a couple of karats. She got the brand-new Cherry M3 BMW. I didn't even have a BMW and I was out here in the trenches every day making sure Bomb in a Bag kept rolling. Dontae takes care of that shiesty ass bitch better than he takes care of the very niggas responsible for getting him enough money to take care of the bitch in the first place. Princess is along for the ride.

I couldn't tell a nigga shit that thought his success meant he knew everything. He would learn about Princess soon enough. I finished directing traffic and jogged over to Princess's Beamer.

I smiled and said, "What's up, Princess?"

She smiled and said, "Hey, Cat Eyes, where is Dontae?"

I shrugged. "He in his skin, when he jumps out, you jump in..."

"Don't play with me, Cat Eyes. Shoo...I'm serious," she said, then she picked up what looked like a Mcdonald's milkshake.

As she wrapped her juicy lips around the straw and started sucking on it. She looked up at me. I felt my dick get hard. That's what I meant about her, Princess was a freak. She would creep with a nigga. All she needed was the right opportunity. I knew her type.

"That shake must be good. What kind is it?" I told her.

She spits the straw out. "Vanilla, I like vanilla," she sang, holding her cup toward me, "Want some?"

I shook my head. "Nall, I'm straight," I told her.

See what I mean? Princess is gon' hurt my nigga in the end. He don't even see it 'cause love got him too blind to see this bitch for who she really is. I would hate for him to learn from her the hard way. She was the kind of bitch that would break bad soon as a nigga was in cuffs, or run off with another nigga and let that other nigga spend your bag after you was dead. Just then, I thought about ways to expose that bitch for who she really was.

Princess looked me up and down. "So, you don't want none of my milkshakes, huh?"

I told her, "I don't like Vanilla, I like Strawberry."

She gazed at me in a freaky way. "I just bet you do," she said, then looked around. "Come on, Cat Eyes. Tell me where Dontae is?"

"I don't know where he is," I told her. "Hit him on the horn." I pulled out a cornsack of weed I'd copped earlier from Don't Believe The Hype, then I pulled out some rollin' papers and rolled a joint.

She said, "I did. He ain't answerin'."

"You paged him?"

"He ain't callin' me back," she said, bringin' a fist down on the steerin' wheel. "I know he somewhere dirty dickin' around with one of them nasty ass project bitches."

I fired up my joint. "I don't think so, Princess," I told her, "You know ever since that shit that happened to Fatso, that nigga Dontae been goin' through a thang. I ain't seen him in a few days either. Ain't nobody seen him. His momma was just down here lookin' for him right before you pulled up."

She held her fingers out. "Lemme hit somthin'?"

I passed the joint to her. She inhaled, then exhaled and coughed. After that, she beat her chest and handed the joint back to me.

"Uh-uh...that's that shit off 47th Street. Ain't it?"

I smiled at her. "Yup."

She frowned. "They runnin' around sayin' them niggas puttin' some shit on that weed. You should stop smokin' that shit."

I told her, "Ain't nothin' wrong with this weed. You just got virgin lungs."

She looked me up and down, rolled her eyes, and smacked her lips.

"Nigga," she said. "Ain't nothin' virgin about me."

I looked at Princess for a moment and I felt the sexual tension between us. She was always flirtatious like this with me. But out of respect for my nigga I had never crossed the line. However, the more she flirted with me, the weaker my defenses became. Princess had a shiny, red, apple in her hand that she had gotten from the serpent.

"Who you been creepin' with lately?" she asked me.

I asked her, "Why you wanna know?"

She shrugged. "I just asked."

"If I tell you, you ain't gon do nothin' but go runnin' to tell Keisha."

Keisha was my main bitch. She, Princess, and Angie were friends, but Keisha wasn't as cool with Princess as Angie was.

"Nigga, please," Princess said. "When have you ever known me to have a big mouth?"

I chuckled. "You know y'all be gettin' together talkin' about us."

"We talk about y'all," she said, confirmin' my belief. "But not how you think. We don't tell each other all our business," she said, then she looked me directly in the eye. "I know how to keep my mouth closed."

I told her, "But a closed mouth don't get fed."

She said, "Luckily for you, I ain't tryna get fed through the mouth. Thank you."

I told Princess she was funny as hell.

Then Sneak interrupted us. They were out of bundles.

"Gon get up outta here, Princess," I told her. "If I see Dontae I'll tell him you was down here lookin' for him."

"You do that," she said, then she sped off.

I shook my head. That bitch Princess was playin' real live games, and I don't even think she knew who she was playing with. Like I said, Dontae had a bad bitch but that bitch ain't shit.

He would find out about her ass soon enough.

CHAPTER 7
DONTAE

Fatso's funeral went down on a gloomy October afternoon. The sky was an angry gray over a misty blue backdrop. The wind was blowing every which way. The city kept it moving like my man wasn't about to be buried today. Saddened about the day's events, I sat outside A.R. Leak's Funeral Home on 76th and Cottage Grove, chainsmoking blunts and drinking a bottle of Remy Martin VSOP, which was my man's favorite drink. I had no desire to go into the funeral service. For one, I preferred to remember Fatso as he was. I didn't want that picture of him, stiff as a mannequin, stuck in my head. When I thought of my man, I wanted that memory to be of my fat homie, fresh as a muhfucka in the latest designer wear, doing the damn thang. For two, I knew there would be a bunch of niggas inside who didn't fuck with folks for real. My nigga was a real muhfucka, and he'd put hands on a lot of fake ass niggas in the projects. The hate for him was always lurking under the surface, and he really didn't fuck with any of the sheisty ass bitches in the projects. To him, all they wanted was a nigga to save 'em. If a nigga didn't you had to worry about them setting the play. I didn't attend Fatso's funeral 'cause everything about it would be fake.

When the service was finally over, everybody filed out and formed a procession in front of the funeral home. I didn't join it. Instead, I allowed the somber caravan to take off. Then I followed, from a few cars behind, 'til the procession reached Oakwood Cemetery.

I drove into the opposite side of the cemetery, parked beside a pond, and crawled out of my Benz with a blunt in one hand and the bottle of Remy in the other. Quietly, I skulked up behind a gothic, cement mausoleum. Sparrows chased each other around in the sky as I smoked, drank, and looked on at the circle standing around Fatso's blue and gold casket. I saw his mother, Ms. Toni with her blonde dreadlocks over her mocha skin, black shades, black coat, black everything. Princess was wearing all black, too and she was holding on to Angie, Fatso's baby momma as she fell apart. Cat Eyes was standing behind the women, his Armani shades gleaming in the blue day.

The preacher, a bulky man in a black suit, dropped ceremonial dirt onto Fatso's flower-covered casket as he said, "Ashes to ashes and dust to dust."

After this everyone dispersed and crawled back into cars. There was no doubt in my mind that from this day forth all of them fake muhfuckas would forget about my nigga. In this city, if you got killed, muhfuckas sparked blunts and forgot you ever existed. When I was sure everyone was gone, I walked out from behind the mausoleum. A sparrow was perched atop a granite headstone. As I walked by it, the sparrow flew away. As soon as I reached Fatso's casket I twisted the cap off the Remy and poured a swig out over the flowers. Then I fired up a blunt and kicked it with my nigga for one last time.

"Aye, Jo', remember when we first met? We was seven years old, and you had stolen a cigarette from yo' old G and smoked it like you'd been smokin' cigarettes since you were two," I said and chuckled. After hitting the blunt and taking swigs off the Remy, I continued, "I hit the cigarette after you, and when I coughed up my lungs, you laughed at me till you was bent over. My nigga, we got our first piece of pussy together, our first bankroll, our first cars...life ain't gon' be the same without you. But check this fly shit out, though," I said, then hit the blunt, took another swig, and said, "I'ma catch the nigga that took you away from me. That's on the love, Jo'. I'ma buss his shit for what he did to you. You got my word on that one. Well, it's gettin' kinda nippy out here, homeboy. Don't worry about Angie and Rashaun. I'll look after

50

them, they gon be a'ight. And Ms. Toni straight, too. Goodbye, my nigga. Rest in peace!" I said, dropped the Remy bottle and the blunt into the six-foot ditch where Fatso would reside 'til Ressurection Day. Then I turned and walked away, vowing not to let my man's death go unpunished.

****

That night I was in the streets again searching for the bitch Streetlight. It had been a week since I started looking for her, and during that week, I'd gotten so preoccupied with finding her, that I hadn't been by the 534 building, I hadn't been home to change my clothes, I hadn't even called Princess to check on her. I had been held up in the Michigan Inn, a raunchy motel, you know the kind of spot with multi-colored doors on 36th and Michigan Ave. Just me, my .40s, and enough rage to burn down a small city.

It was well after 11:00 p.m. when I finally spotted Streetlight. She was standing in front the Rothschild's Liquor store off 39th and Indiana, The Ave. The parkin' lot was crowded, but I could still see her. She was rocking a strawberry blonde wig with a lotta inches, it crashed into her dark skin like a head-on collision. The rest of the bitch was covered and threatening to bust out of her red maxi and tight blue jeans. A pair of red come fuck me pumps and matching handbag rounded off her ensemble. I checked her out for a moment. Thought about tricking off with her cause I hadn't busted a nut in a week. But that thought dissipated like smoke in a strong wind. I was here for information. Not a nut, a nut I could get any time. This visit was about finding Reggie Wade.

A crowd of niggas in black hoodies with bulges in their waists crossed the street as I pulled into the crowded liquor store's parking lot. I had put The Benz up and jumped into my low-key black-on-black 72 Cutlass Supreme with chrome dual exhaust pipes. That bitch had some shit under the hood, and it growled like a fierce lion.

I eased on the breaks as I pulled up beside Streetlight. When I came to a full stop, I rolled my window down and said, "Aye, Jo, you tryna go out on a date?"

I used the classic trick-off language. In the city of Chicago whenever a nigga pulled up on a ho and asked her to go out on a date. The ho knew she had her a trick. From that point, the ho might tell the nigga to show her his dick to prove he wasn't the twist. Streetlight didn't do that to me. She just let her eyes touch me and the entire interior of my vehicle.

Then she asked as she chewed hard on bubble gum, "Do I know you, sweetie?"

I smiled, then told her, "Nall, you don't know me yet, Jo', but I know you."

She kept chewing her bubble gum. "How you know me?" She had a skeptical look on her face.

I answered, "Are you serious? You kiddin' me right now, right? Everybody on The Low-End knows you got the best head from State Street to the Lake."

The Low-End was the lower Southside area. It ran from 22nd to 55th Street and State Street to Lake Michigan.

"I'm just tryna see if all the hype is true."

Streetlight blew a bubble, causing it to burst. Then she took the gum, straightened it with her index finger, and wrapped the gum around her tongue. When she was done, she winked at me and said, "Yes, sweetie, the hype is oh so true. The question is how much you tryna pay to find out?"

I told her to hop in, to get our business off Front Street and she ran around the back of the Cutlass with her Maxi and jeans struggling to keep her fat ass contained. I popped the locks and she hopped into the passenger seat. She was an amazon, the Cutlass gave to her weight. The smell of lavender perfume over pussy permeated the car. I tasted the odor on my tongue. That caused me to leave a crack in the window when I rolled it up. I pulled out of the parking lot of the liquor store before she could shut the passenger door.

She asked me, "Ain't you that ole' boy who runs that Bomb in a Bag dope line?"

I told her, "Yeah, that's me." Then I asked, "Where you tryna go?"

She told me to bend the block and come around on 37th Street.

We ended up in the gravel parking lot, across the street from Home of the Champs, a famous pool hall on The Ave. The spot was famous 'cause it had hosted big money games between the big players in the city. Back in the day, a nigga could sit outside and watch kingpins like Flukie Stokes, Marlo Cole and Larry Porter crawl out of limos draped in enough diamonds and gold to clothe an Egyptian Pharoah. Minnesota Fats, one of the best pool sharks in the country had even played at the spot. But tonight, dope fiends and winos was blowing up and down the strip like litter in the wind, and every now and then, an old dusty groove by Isaac Hayes or The Iceman Jerry Butler would escape the joint as its door opened to spit out a loser.

I parked and killed the engine.

Streetlight turned toward me in her seat and became 110% business. "Kay, sweetie," she said with honey dripping from her tongue. "I'ma give you a couple of cracks at it for a half-a-sleeve. You gon' need a couple of cracks at it. Please believe me. If I don't suck that dick twice you gon feel like I beat outta yo lil money," she said, took her purse off her shoulder, and sat it on the floor. Then she looked at me and told me, "Kay, sweetie, pull that dick out. I wanna see what I'm workin' with."

She smiled at me hard.

I told her, "I ain't tryna get my dick sucked."

Her smile stayed hard. "Oh," she said. "That's fine. You must want some of this sweet black pussy, then?"

"Nall, I'm straight," I told her. "I ain't really tryna trick-off with you at all."

Her smile cracked and hit the floor. "What you want then, sweetie? I ain't got time for games. You better start talkin', or I'm walkin'," all the honey in her voice turned to vinegar.

I told her, "I think you got some info I'm meant for."

She checked her watch, it was one of them cheap metal, stretch band muhfuckas that'd turn your wrist green in a couple of days.

"My time is precious, sweetie," she said with her hand on the door handle.

"I'll pay you for your time. I just need to ask you a few questions."

I watched her look around like she was nervous or impatient, or both. I could've sworn she wanted to tell me to go fuck myself, 'til I reached in my jeans and pulled out a crispy Ben Franklin. I handed it to her. She snatched it, held it up to the light. I guess she was satisfied with the $100 bill authenticity, 'cause after holdin' it to the light she folded it and stuck it down between her huge titties.

Then she cracked her window, pulled out a soft pack of Newports and a Bic. After that, she fired up and asked, "What you wanna know?"

"Tell me where I can find Reggie Wade?"

The bitch looked me straight in the eye and said, "I don't know nobody name, Reggie Wade."

I took a deep breath. It took everything I had in me to stop me from hauling off and slapping the taste out of the bitch's mouth. The bitch was telling me a bald-faced lie, and I knew it. I wasn't green, I had been in the streets long enough to pick the greatest liar out of a crowd of known liars. See, the streets had a lot of different liars. Some of them were harmless. The other ones fell into a few recognizable categories. You had the beat-out liar. This was the liar that couldn't look you in the eyes while conducting some kind of business. He was so easily detected 'cause you could see lie written all over him. Next, there was the liar that lied to make himself seem like more than what he really was. These kinds of liars got exposed whenever they were asked to produce proof. Occasionally, you ran into the liar who could look you directly in the eye and make you believe you didn't see some shit you had just seen with yo' own eyes. Streetlight was this kind of liar, but all niggas in the streets got a little liar in 'em. You needed it to survive.

I spun on her with my top lip curled exposing my fangs. "Bitch, don't play with me."

She sunk in her seat, and her cigarette became the most important thing to her.

I told the bitch, "I know you used to fuck with the nigga some type of way cause somebody put me on yo bumper, jo…"

"Who?" she blurted like she'd really like to know where I got my information.

"That's a whole other conversation, but check this fly shit out, jo'? All you need to know is I'm willin' to do anything to get the answers to my questions." What I said made her look at me again.

When that bitch's eyes were on mine, I slid my hand into the pocket of my jacket. I let her see the monster that lived in me again. That monster was angry, vengeful, and desperate. A tense moment crept into the car like the grim reaper. He showed his chrome scythe and vanished after promisin' to come back for us both.

Streetlight smoked her cigarette down to the filter, then thumped it out through the crack in her window. After that, she turned to me and said, "I ain't seen Reggie since he been out, sweetie. Honest, and to keep it real with you I ain't tryna see him. If you lookin' for him you already know that nigga is a million different kinds of crazy. I don't need his bullshit in my life. Besides, I know he holdin' on to some type of animosity towards me."

"Why?" I asked her.

She shrugged. "How would I know why that crazy ass nigga feels the way he feels? I just know we was fuckin' around before he went to the joint. I guess he expected me to do that bid with his ass."

I sat there thinking about what Streetlight was saying. I knew this was the way a lot of bitches felt when it came to holding on to relationships with niggas in prison. Yet, I'd never heard the shit so raw. Her words made me think about me and Princess. Would we last if I had to go to prison?

"I stopped acceptin' his collect calls, and I stopped answerin' his letters. I moved on with my life. Honest, I was happy that nigga was in the joint. And I know that shit sound fucked up cause you ain't 'posed to wish prison on yo' worst enemy. But I'm keepin' it real. Him goin' to the joint gave me the strength to do some shit I should've done a long time ago."

"And what was that?" I asked.

Streetlight wrung her fingers and said, "Leave him."

I looked at the bitch and checked her for the lie. She passed my smell test and that put me on the block between St. Elsewhere and St. Nowhere. Yet and still, I kept the press on her, "How long was y'all fuckin' around?"

She fired up another cigarette and was like, "We fucked around off and on since we was teenagers. He took me to prom and everything. I loved the shit outta that nigga's dirty draws, but that was before he started goin' in and outta jail. He ain't the same dude he was back then. Honest, sweetie. Now that I look back on it, his elevator ain't never ran all the way up to the top floor. But out here in these streets, it makes a bitch feel safe to have a nigga every other nigga fears. I know you understand that?"

I did. My old man had been a gunslinger. He protected me and my mother with his life, but, in the end, his gunslingin' had failed him. He had been unable to protect his own life. There was no question that niggas had gazed upon my old man with fear. His

56

death made me question how far fear really got a muhfucka in the streets.

I looked over at the pool hall. It was still spittin' out losers to dusty grooves. To my left, I could see the well-lit intersection at 39th and Indiana gettin' busier. Candy-colored lights bathed the grime and grit of the city. The hawk blew hard enough to scoot the Cutlass over one space.

I turned to Streetlight again. "All I need to know is where I can find him?"

"I don't know, sweetie. Honest," she said before she thumped another cigarette out of the window. "Like I told you, I ain't seen him. And I don't wanna see him. I can't tell you where to find him, but I can tell you how."

My spidey senses tingled. "How?" I asked on the edge of my seat.

She told me, "Keep askin' people where you can find him and he'll find you."

I took what she just me and turned it around in my head a few times. It didn't take me long to figure out what she was trying to tell me. She was saying if I turned over enough rocks I'd find the snake. It was some threat in her words. I heard some warning in them, too. Her words were like a smoke alarm beeping before you saw the fire. I took her cue 'cause I knew from experience you had to be careful turning over rocks. If I was gonna turn them over, I knew I'd better be ready to kill the snake. Without a doubt, the second that snake rock was turned over it'd be poised to strike anything in striking distance.

"I'm sorry about your friend, sweetie. Honest," Steetlight said as she repeatedly rubbed her palms across the thighs of her jeans. "But that's all the info I got for you. You do look a little tense, though. Why don't you go ahead and pull that dick out and lemme tighten you up?" she offered.

I seriously considered her offer for a quick tick and decided she was right. I was tense as a rope stretched to the max. I unbuckled, unzipped, and pulled my dick out.

Then I laid my seat back and got comfortable.

Streetlight leaned over to my seat, grabbed the head of my dick, and held it with both hands like a trophy.

"Damn, sweetie, this dick already rock hard. And it got the nerve to be big, too," she said as she licked on my dick to wet it. "I bet yo' lil' girlfriend love this big ol' dick. Umm-hmmm...she do, but honest, sweetie, I bet you she can't suck this dick better than I can," she bragged as she massaged my hard dick with both hands.

I told her, "You shole talkin' a good one."

She fired back, "Watch this."

She turned that dick sideways and swallowed me like a whale swallowing a guppy. When she bobbed upward, she squeezed me between both her palms, twisting in opposite directions, and flicking her wet tongue across the hole in the tip of my dick. Her technique sent shivers up my spine. She repeated this technique for about a minute. As soon as the tip of my hard dick became swollen and sensitive, she squeezed me harder, massaged my balls with her other hand, and sucked me like the last of a drink she was gulping through a straw. I busted a nut that burned good on the way out. My entire body trembled. I grabbed a hand full of her wig and held her in place 'til my spasms stopped.

She spit me out, smiled, and told me, "You ain't last a minute with this head."

I told her, "You cheated."

"What?" she blurted, looking offended.

"You used both hands," I told her. "Try that shit again with no hands?"

She chuckled. "It ain't gon' be the same."

I told the bitch, "I know it, you cheated."

She said, "You wanna try again?"

"Hell yeah."

I tried that shit again. A counselor at the Audy Homes, the juvenile jail in the city had told me the definition of insanity is doing the same thing over and over and expecting different results. I must've been insane, then, 'cause I'd let Streetlight suck my dick again, and the result had come out the same as the first time she'd sucked it. I lasted one minute.

She winked at me and said, "I'm great, ain't I?"

"You can bottle that shit and sell it for fifty-nine-ninety-nine."

She laughed for a moment. Then got herself together and climbed out of the car.

Before she closed the door, she told me, "You know what, sweetie? Reggie used to run with the Dirty Snatchers back in the day. The gang might be a little bit before your time, but I know you heard of' em."

I had, everybody on The Low-End had heard of The Dirty Snatchers. They were the Ali Baba and the Forty Thieves of The Low-End. They robbed, stole, and pillaged their way into street history in the early 80s for running roughshod over crews like The Bogus Boyz and The Del Vikings. They were closer to crews like the C-note Mafia, The Gangsta Goon Squad, and The Casias. A nigga who went by the name Dirtybird was the crew's ringleader. I'd seen him in Ellis Park not too long ago, selling merch with a thief bitch named Gloria. GLO was a Cannon, and a Cannon did everything from short and long cons to picking pockets and bussing checks. If you caught the right Cannon, you could cop a new life, which came with a brand-new driver's license and credit cards.

Dirty Bird had settled with Glo'. He wasn't dirty snatching no more.

I told Streetlight I knew some of the Dirty Snatchers, but I didn't know Reggie Wade was one of them.

"Yeah, sweetie," she answered. "He ran with them niggas, but most 'em ain't runnin' too much of nowhere no more. Most of em dead or in prison. The ones that ain't is strung out." She closed the lapels of her Maxi coat against The Hawk. "If you're serious about findin' Reggie you'll start with the Dirty Snatchers. Dirty

Bird, Sky, and Stretcher is still around somewhere. I don't know about the rest of 'em."

I thanked Streetlight for putting that lil bug in my ear. She told me not to say where it came from. I promised her I wouldn't, and she slammed the passenger door shut, then sashayed away, hiking her red handbag higher up on her shoulder. I sat there for a moment, watching her big ass sway side to side as she made her way up The Ave. I was almost beginning to wonder what that pussy was like when she disappeared around the corner at 38th Street. I needed to get my ass home to Princess tonight. After all, Streetlight had hit me with some valuable information I could follow up on. My work in these cold streets was done for now. As I started the Cutlass the door of the pool hall flew open. I heard Curtis Mayfield sing some of The Other Side of Town. Then I saw a humongous nigga with a head the size of a cinderblock, toss a slim nigga, head-first, out onto the sidewalk. The slim nigga got to his feet, used his Kangol to dust himself off, then stumbled into a smooth walk up The Ave. I felt like that slim nigga. My spot had been robbed. My nigga Fatso had been killed. The shit had tossed me out on my head, but I was back on my feet.

Now, there was hell to pay.

CHAPTER 8
REGGIE WADE

I had been held up with the bitch Mi-Mi for a week straight. The lil punk, bitch had fucked me and sucked me dry and in the process, she'd helped me blow through that lil' merch I'd stained them vics for in the 534 building. I had woken up the late-night, eyes running, stomach doing somersaults, bones, and joints aching, body feeling like I'd just went a couple of rounds with Iron Mike Tyson. That dope sickness was kicking in. I had a few old gunshot wounds that gave me hell. The pain was unbearable. I could hardly move if I didn't have any dope in me. I had to hit the streets tonight. The last time I'd suffered the twin pains that came from my gunshot wounds and being dope sick, I shitted myself. You ever seen a grown man shit himself? I promise you, it's not a pretty sight. After that happened, I swore that I'd run through hell with gasoline draws on before I allowed myself to be that sick again. Any nigga that stood in between me and whatever it was I needed to keep that dope Jones off me was a dead nigga.

Straight like that.

By the time I had pulled myself out of Mi-Mi's hot ass pussy and pried her fingers off this dick, it was well after midnight, which just so happened to be my time of night. I jumped into my gear and walked out of Mi-Mi's crib as the blackness of night fell on the Ida B. Wells like a casket top. My state of awareness was high when I started marching through my stomping grounds. I allowed my paranoid eyes to touch every hallway, every corner, and every courtyard while navigating the maze of rowhouse buildings on my way toward Cottage Grove. For me, to be aware was to be alive. A nigga could never be too careful in the streets. Especially a nigga who'd made as many enemies as me. When you lived life like mines, murder was always in a ski mask and leather gloves, lurkin' in dark hallways, peeking around corners, and selling you death on an ice-cold wind.

Now I had a new enemy, a faceless enemy, for whom I had to be on point. Out here, enemies turned into quick footsteps behind a nigga, and a couple sizzling hot balls in the back of the head. I had to do everything in my power to keep that from happening to me. I didn't have enough fingers and toes to count how many times I'd heard about a nigga getting his shit split after he'd just touched down from the joint.

Dontae. This was the name of my faceless enemy. The nigga bothered my thoughts like a muhfucka. But that was a fresh beef. It could hold. I had some old beef on the stove that needed cooking before it spoiled and that beef's name was Iroc Tony.

Before I went to the joint, Iroc Tony shot me with a Mac .90. He hit me twice, one in the gut and one in the hip. The bullet I'd taken in the gut burned through my lower intestines, busted out of my ribs, and crashed into my forearm. That bitch ass shit put me in a shitbag for six months and shattered the bone of my forearm so bad that it had to be replaced with a metal rod. The other bullet cracked my hip bone, and it took me months to get back on my feet. The whole thing left me with a limp and so many scars that I looked like the victim of a vicious shark attack. Every time it rained I thought about Iroc Tony. When it rained the pain from the wounds, he'd inflicted became excruciating. They gave me pain meds in the hospital and pain meds in prison, but I was unable to afford pain meds in the free world, so my dope habit got worse. I was spending $15,000 a month on heroin. I was feeding a gorilla who was constantly growing, and whenever he was hungry, he beat on my back like a bass drum. All this shit was Iroc Tony's fault. The nigga had fucked me up something crucial. However, he hadn't finished the job, he should've. I won't make that same mistake with him.

I took to a dark hallway in a rowhouse building on Cottage Grove. It smelled like wet newspaper and cat piss, but I ignored the foul odor. I had been in prison for five years, smelling other niggas' bad breath, musty armpits, and stinkin' ass feet. Occasionally, I'd even accidentally walked into a shower stall, where a nigga had just fucked a punk in the ass so hard that he'd shit on the shower's tiled floor. I had smelled foul odors in my life, so the smell in the hallway didn't faze me.

I posted up in the darkness, and on my box of Newports I laid out a bag of dope and finished it off with one nostril. I felt a medicine drain almost immediately. After that, I licked a finger, cleaned my nose, licked that finger, then fired up a square. The menthol smoke set the party off right. Now, I was ready to work.

From where I stood, I could see O.T.'s Meat Market, an Arab store that sold everything from hog head cheese and condoms to liquor and crackpipes. Niggas stumbled in and spilled out of the joint as wine heads held the wall up and held out hands that resembled panhandling cups.

"Aye, big money, you know you clownin' em out here. Look out for the cookout?"

"Boss Boss, I'm slow gettin' em and po' hittin' em. You got some spare change?"

"Chief, you shole look good tonight. Lemme get a Shortie White outta ya. It's only a dollar."

"I ain't had a wine tonight, pretty lady. Mines only cost seventy-five cents."

I turned my nose up in disgust. I never understood how a nigga reduced himself to begging when there was scratch all over the streets. I had never begged a nigga for shit. I had never liked the idea that if I asked, a nigga had the right to tell me no. Taking what I wanted had always made more sense than begging to me.

I looked over at the parkin' lot between the store and the rowhouse building across the street. Behind this was Newtown, Iroc Tony's stompin' ground. A couple of days after I'd hit the bricks, I'd fell through Dirty Bird's crib and he told me Iroc Tony was layin' his head on the 4th Floor of the first building, behind O.T.'s Meat Market. Dirty Bird was an old road dog of mine and I knew I could trust his information, so I was out tonight to act upon it. I needed to see Iroc Tony's ass and make my face the last face he saw.

In order to get this accomplished, I had to get into Newtown. I knew I couldn't just walk across the street. If I did that I'd be a seven-footer in a party full of midgets. That goofy shit would surely get me killed. Quickly, I thought of a better entrance. I took one last pull off my square and thumped it to the ground. It bounced and sparked on the cold pavement as I walked back around the rowhouse building and marched through the empty courtyards. Before I reached 38th Place I walked up on three niggas in Triple Fat Goose coats, shootin' dice on a hallway stoop. I surprised them with The Beast.

They looked at me and froze like Simon Says.

"Y'all know what this is," I told them vics. "Leave everything y'all got on the stoop. And run—" I pointed west. "—that way. And don't stop till y'all get to Vincennes."

The vics dug in and came up off jewelry, crack bundles, and scratch. They sat that shit on the stoop with the dice pot and took off.

Boom!

I fired a warnin' shot and they got low and ran faster. After that, I scooped up the merch and continued my trek to Newtown. See what you come across when you ain't begging? It's scratch all over the streets.

The first building. The people who lived in the Madden Park Homes called this building the office building cause the project's administration work was done on the 1st Floor of this building. That was during the day. As for right now, the 10-story building was dark and dry. Wasn't a fool in sight so I skulked into the joint and headed straight for the stairwell. As soon as I crept into the stairwell, a naked bulb started blinking and buzzing like a dying insect. The stairs were wet, the red walls were sweating and the air smelled like orange disinfectant over vomit and piss. I climbed the staircase, and on the third floor, a lighter sparked. After that, I spotted a spidery couple hittin' a sizzlin' crack pipe.

I kept it movin'. I had somethin' to smoke tonight and it wasn't crack.

On the 4th Floor, I found a vacant apartment. I high stepped over piles of trash, found a crate, and turned it upside down. Then I settled in for the wait. Iroc Tony had put me in a shitbag. That muhfucka had been uncomfortable as hell. I still gagged thinking about it. He'd also left me with a limp and that shit fucked up my mobility. I was a little banged up, but the nigga had fucked up and let me live. Now, I was poised to make that the worst mistake he'd ever made in his life.

My bad wheel had gone to sleep by the time I finally heard keys on the 4th Floor porch. I rubbed my leg down to get the blood back circulating. It felt like a hive of bees stinging my shit when I got to my feet. I peeked out the door of the vaco and spotted Iroc Tony fumblin' with a ring-full of keys. It was him, he was a little heavier than I remembered, but it was definitely him. He was wearin' a black Sherling, blue jeans, and Vangrack's. I got a good look at his profile and felt a sudden rush of adrenaline. I popped out on him with The Beast.

His eyes jumped out of his head. His ring full of keys hit the cement.

I covered the space between us like I didn't have a bad wheel. I got close enough to him to smell his fear. He passed gas and I smelled it in the wind. My top lip curled up as I glared grimly at him from behind the scarred nose of The Beast. I heard piss tricklin' down his leg.

I saw that shit soak the front of his jeans.

"Is that piss, Tony?" I teased, as I smiled deviously.

Iroc Tony didn't blink. He just swallowed hard and said, "Reg-Reg-Reggie, Sky told me that shit between us was squashed."

Sky was one of my 8-track-niggas another one of my Dirty Snatcher homies. He was just as shiesty and thirsty as they came. There was no doubt in my mind that he told Iroc Tony he would squash our beef for a little piece of change. If Iroc Tony believed that shit, I had a Building to sell him downtown.

I shook my head. "I don't know what Sky told you. But Sky can't squash no shit for me. He ain't my spokesman. I take care of my own business in these streets, vic," I said, then I gritted on the nigga 'til he trembled.

"C'mon, Reggie," Iroc Tony pleaded. "You here to settle some shit from five years ago, Jo?"

I kept The Beast in his face. "Vic, I wouldn't give a fuck if the shit happened five centuries ago. Scars for scabs. You know the lick."

I stared into his eyes, I could see his mind workin' to come up with an out.

After a nerve-rackin' couple seconds, he said, "I tell you what," he said this like he was about to try to sell me a lemon. "I got a lil piece of change in the crib. Lemme give you this shit? After that, we can part ways and forget this ever happened."

For a fast second, I thought about his offer. The shit didn't need much considerin'. I had always believed it was better to go in a vic pockets before I split his wig. A vic mighta been holdin' on to my bond money.

After turnin' his offer upside down to see what was under it, I poked him in his head with the nose of The Beast. The blow was hard enough to leave two perfect circles imprinted on his forehead.

"Pick the keys up, vic," I barked through clenched teeth. "Let's finish this in the crib."

Slowly, Iroc Tony kneeled and picked up his keys. He fumbled with 'em long enough to piss me off. I chopped him across the back of the head with the barrel of The Beast. A loud yell leaped out of his mouth as he flew face-first into the door of apartment 406. That chop made him find the right key. He opened the door. I walked him into the dark hallway of the apartment with a fist full of his Sherling, and the barrel of The Beast in his back.

One false move and I'd open his back up so wide a full-grown man would be able to climb through his ass.

I kicked the door shut behind me and asked, "Anybody else in here, vic?"

Iroc Tony nodded. "My bitch probably in the bedroom sleep. C'mon, Jo, you ain't gotta do it like this," he whimpered. "Just lemme go in the room and get you that lil' piece of change. I ain't gon' try shit, I swear to God—"

"*God! God!* Don't gimmie that God shit! Muhfuckas always wanna remember God when they 'bouta get they shit split. Bitch ass nigga. You think I'm slow? If I let you go in that room, you comin' out blazin'. And you wouldn't even be wrong. You got the right plan. You just got the wrong man."

Iroc Tony's shoulders fell. "I just don't want this shit to get outta hand, Jo. That's all."

"Well, if you don't want it to get outta hand, act like it. No surprises, vic. I mean it. You try any bullshit, and I'm leavin' you, and that bitch in this muhfucka stankin'. Straight like that."

I used the barrel of The Beast to poke Iroc Tony through the dark hallway. The other end of the hallway let out into a huge living room with black leather sectional, glass tables, strobe lamps, and a 5,000 dollar entertainment system. All this shit was situated as perfectly as a furniture store display on top of a red, black, and gold Persian rug. I loved what Iroc Tony had done with the place. The shit looked good, but it wouldn't for that much longer. I was about to redecorate this shit with blood and guts. Skillfully, I flipped The Beast around like a baton and whacked Iroc Tony across the back of his head with its butt, opening up a six-inch gash to the white meat. The impact sent him crashing face-first into the floor.

He was out cold.

I left him unconscious on the living room floor and ran into his bedroom. In there, the shape of a thick bitch was outlined under a plush, down comforter. I snatched the comforter back and in the moonlight spilling through the bedroom window I could see her naked curves. She was in red-laced panties. They looked good on her chocolate skin. Her perky titties were bare. They looked like honeydews with raisins on the ends. A colorful, silk scarf was wrapped around her head. Iroc Tony's bitch looked like an African queen.

Too bad she had to die. Her fault for fuckin with a bitch ass nigga like Iroc Tony. Her eyes fluttered open and as soon as she realized I wasn't her man, they bugged, and her mouth opened wide for a scream. I stuck the barrel of The Beast right inside. It broke teeth on the way in and muffled the bitch's screams.

"Outta bed, bitch," I told her as I held The Beast steady in her mouth. "We goin' in the living room."

She blinked and tears fell down her cheeks. Then she sat up, crawled out of bed, and let me steer her, back first, into the living room. I yanked The Beast outta her mouth. She spit half her fronts out and screamed. I hit her across the head with the barrel and knocked her ass out like her man.

By the time, the two of them came to, I had rambled through the apartment and found extension cords and phone cords and bound them tightly at the wrists and ankles. I walked over to the entertainment system and with a leather-gloved finger, I turned on the stereo. *Assassin* by *The Geto Boys* blared from the speakers. When I walked back over to the bloody couple, I sat down on the sectional, across from them, and pointed The Beast in their direction. They looked at me in fear. I took a bath in that shit like it was steaming hot water.

"Oh, my God!" Iroc Tony's bitch cried. "Please don't kill us."

I looked at her. She wasn't so pretty anymore, all bloody and snagga tooth, and shit.

Her kinda scared, a nigga only witnessed in haunted houses.

I lowered The Beast. "Your man ain't tell you he shot me?" I grumbled.

She shook her head. "No, he didn't." She looked at Iroc Tony. "Why you shoot him, Tony?"

Iroc Tony had a look on his face that said he'd rather be sliding down a razor blade into a pool of rubbing alcohol than to be having this conversation. "I shot him cause he robbed me, Nikki. He stuck me up and took my last. But that shit was five years ago. If you still tryna get that lil' piece of change, it's in the dresser on the right side of the bedroom. All you gotta do is pull the bottom drawer out. It's twenty thousand in there. It's all yours. Take it and go."

I used The Beast as a cane to help me get to my feet. Then I took a couple of steps that placed me over Iroc Tony and his bitch. "You tellin' me what to do now, Tony?" I snarled.

He bitched up. "Of course, not, I was just sayin'. You want that lil' piece of change, don't you?"

He had a point. I nodded. "Yeah, Tony," I mumbled. "Yeah, I do want that lil piece of change."

I swung The Beast upward and the barrel came to rest on my right shoulder. A sound escaped the lips of Iroc Tony bitch that reminded me of a car stalling. I ignored this, spun on my heels about-face, and disappeared into the bedroom.

The scratch was behind the bottom draw in an orange Nike shoe box. I ditched the box and stuffed the scratch in my pockets. Then walked back into the living room and found the bloody love birds having a whisper conversation. That shit stopped as soon as they realized I was back in the room. I hoped they were saying their last I- love-yous cause like Saran this shit was a wrap.

I nodded slowly. "Iroc Tony, I fucks with you,vic. You keep it all the way real," I told him. "Now where the dope and the guns?"

"Huh?" he grunted.

"You heard me, muhfucka," I growled. "Where the dope and the guns. Cause I ain't gon' feel safe in the streets 'lest you completely popped, vic," I said that to trick him into a false sense of security.

That shit wasn't nothin' but the overplay for the underplay. There was no way I was leaving him and his bitch in here alive. Deep down, Iroc Tony looked like he knew that, but he had to trust me. What other choice did he have?

For a moment, Iroc Tony weighed his options. He got to where I was slowly.

He told me, "Ain't no dope and guns in here."

I aimed The Beast at his bitch. "Lie to me again, vic, and I'ma knock this bitch head off her shoulders."

His bitch cried, "Just give him that shit, Tony! Give him all that shit so he can go."

"Shut up, Nikki!" Iroc Tony yelled. "If I give him the shit or not he gon' still kill us!"

He was right, but I didn't give him a yay or nay.

I just told him, "You got a choice, vic. You can hold out and make this shit a lil' more slow and painful, or you can break bread now and get it over with fast," I said, then walked over to the stereo and turned it up to the max. *NWA's Appetite For Destruction* leaped out of the speakers and ran around the living room naked and screaming.

I walked back over to the bloody lovebirds. "It makes no difference to me what you choose to do, I get mine regardless."

Iroc Tony looked at me, and I recognized the defeat in his eyes. He told me everything I was looking for was in a compartment under the entertainment system.

I walked through a spot on the Persian rug where blood and piss had soaked through. That shit squished under my boot. At the entertainment system, I squatted down on my haunches and inspected the grooves of the cabinets. If I didn't know a compartment was there, I would've surely missed it. I ran my fingers along the bottom of the cabinets and I felt a metal lever. I pulled it, and a thin chest slid out. In the thin chest there was about twenty Bomb in a Bag bundles, the same shit I'd taken from the 534 building. A quick thought about Dontae streaked through my mind and disappeared around the corner. Two brand new Desert Eagles with four extra clips sat around the bundles.

I pulled out a black trash bag and collected the bundles. Then I stuck each Desert Eagle into either side of my waistband, then stuffed the clips into the pocket of my trench coat. Everything fit like a dick between two tits.

The Beast helped me get back to my feet. I walked back over to the lovebirds. "Is this everything, vic?" I asked Iroc Tony.

He squirmed around like the worm he was. "You got everything," he whimpered.

I took a long hard look at him, and couldn't determine if he was lyin' or not. But it didn't matter to me either way. I'd already realized that I'd gotten more than I bargained for.

Even a hungry lion knew when he had his fill. Feeling like I'd been in the apartment too long, I snatched a pillow off the sectional and placed it on the back of Iroc Tony's head. He squirmed more, but I put a knee in his back to hold him still. Then, I placed the business end of The Beast on the pillow.

His bitch cried, "No—please—no!"

Iroc Tony screamed, "Come on, Reggie! You ain't gotta do this, Jo. You got everything!"

I told him, "You know this wasn't about the scratch, vic. You fucked me up royally, Tony. But you shoulda played for keeps."

"Please, Reggie! Please don't kill me!" Iroc Tony begged.

"So long, Tony," I told him. "Scars for scabs, vic."

"Wait!" Iroc Tony yelled.

Boom!

I pulled the trigger under the heavy bassline of NWA. The disk slug blasted through the pillow, slammed into Iroc Tony's head, and splattered blood and brains all over the pretty, Persian rug. Iroc Tony was still convulsing when I placed what was left of the pillow over his bitch's head.

She screamed.

Boom!

I pulled the trigger, cutting her scream short.

The slug blasted through the pillow and blew her pretty face all over Iroc Tony. Cushions fell on me like the first snow of winter.

The living room smelled like gunpowder and bodily fluids. *Scarface's Born Killer* blasted out of the speakers. I took a seat on the sectional, reached into the trash bag, pulled out a bundle of dope. Then opened the bundle, busted down a couple of bags on the back of my gloved hand, and took two huge snorts. The dope rushed up to my brain and in seconds, the euphoria I felt almost made me buss a nut.

I fired up a square and bobbed my head to the music.

Born Killer.

That was me. I'd been taking lives since I was a shorty. For as far back as I could remember I'd always been fascinated with blood and guts. People were created with certain talents.

Mine was killing.

The Lord giveth, Reggie Wade taketh away.

I got to my feet and poured the rest of the bundle out onto Iroc Tony and his bitch. Drug-related murders. We'll see how much of the city's resources the twist will be willing to waste on this shit.

CHAPTER 9

DONTAE

The sun beat me in the crib this mornin' after my little conversation with Streetlight. She'd put some serious fat on my head. So, to process it all I'd ridden around the city for a few hours, chain smokin' blunts in silence. Reggie Wade had been one of the Dirty Snatchers, that band of thieves and robbers had pillaged the land like Ghengis Khan and his Mongol army. Sky and Stretcher and the ringleader Dirty Bird was still around. I would have to see about them. No stone would be left unturned when it came to findin' the nigga that had violated me and bussed my nigga's shit.

But I had to be careful in executing my plans. Streetlight's warnin' was constantly playing like a scratched album on the record player of mind. *"I can't tell you where to find him, but I can tell you how. Keep askin' people where to find him, and he'll find you."*

We'll see. First thing was first, I needed a shower, some pussy, and somethin' to eat. After that, I'd sleep for a while, get up and get back on my mission.

Apartment 1109, I keyed myself into my sanctuary. The color scheme was ridiculous, all shades from chocolate to beige. The living room was on some modern art shit. Princess put her twist on the place. If she liked it, I loved it.

I turned into the hallway, before I took two steps toward the bedroom, Princess popped up out of nowhere. She was wearin' an emerald-green, silk robe. The sash was tied tight around her curvy hips. Her pretty toes had French tips like her fingernails.

I smiled.

She didn't.

She looked me up and down like I was day-old doo-doo and said, "Look at what the cat drug in." She folded her arms over her titties. That was her fightin' stance. She didn't need her hands to fight. Her mouth was good enough.

I took a deep breath and told her, "Not right now, Princess. On the real, Jo."

She snapped, *"Not right now! Not right now!* You come up in here after being M.I.A. for a whole week, and you tell me not right now? Fatso done got killed! His funeral done came and went! Everybody askin' me if I've seen you! You done had me stressin' out and shit! I page you, I blow up yo' phone, I been by the five-three-four building lookin' for you! I called the county jail, the county hospital, the county morgue! And you tell me not right now!" She ran up on me and got in my face.

I turned my face to the right and there she was. I turned my face to the left, and there she was.

"That pussy must've been real fire, mister! That head must've been crucial!"

I told her, "You tweakin', Jo'. For real." I tried to walk away.

She pushed me and held me between her and the wall. "You ain't got nothin' to say for yourself, mister!" She shouted. "Nothin'!"

"What you want me to say?" I asked her. "You already got your mind made up about what a muhfucka was doin'," I said that and shrugged. "So, what's the point?"

"Dontae," she said, sizing me up like she was about to steal on me. "Ain't nobody tryna hear that shit. You know you got some explainin' to do."

I looked her in the eye. The only other time I'd seen her this mad was when I'd asked her to use her Honda Civic, and when I gave it back she'd found an empty condom wrapper on the floor.

I took another deep breath.

Princess clapped her hands once and brought them down to her waist. "Let's go, mister," she said. "I'm listenin'."

I just stood there with my head down. Princess was blowin' me. She was amped up. Her hazel eyes were throwing butcher knives at my head. All five-foot-three and 135 pounds of her was in the *and what* stance. Her anger was justified, but I was too exhausted to fight with her ass.

So, I leaned against the wall and tried to reason with her, "Princess, look, I'll talk to you about this shit later. Right now, I'm tired as a muhfucka, bae. I just want a shower, some pussy, and somethin' to eat—in that order."

She shook her head. "Nall, mister, we gon talk now or you can forget about the last two things on that want list."

I pushed her out of the way and left her standin' in the hallway. The last week had been hectic: I'd been robbed, my nigga Fatso had been killed, and I'd had to bury him. On top of all that, I'd been out in the streets looking for a nigga that was like a solar eclipse. I was taking a long, hot shower right now whether Princess liked it, or not.

Fuck it.

I'd deal with her ass later.

I made for the bathroom, but before I was able to walk inside, I heard Princess run up behind me. Then I felt her push the back of my head so hard I hit my chin on my chest and bit my tongue. It took everything in me not to haul off and knock the shit out of her ass. I knew if I hit her now, I'd probably break her jaw. So, I gave her the free one.

She told me, "You been out in the streets all that time. I know you been laid up with one of them dirty ass project bitches. I don't know why I put up with yo' shit," she said, then spun on her heels and disappeared into the bedroom.

I blew out my anger, walked into the bathroom, slammed the door shut, and locked it. I had to get the last week off me before I dealt with Princess.

After my shower, I walked into the bedroom naked and found Princess sitting on the edge of the bed. She had pulled all her shoulder-length hair to her left side and was twisting it with both hands repeatedly. Her right thigh was crossed high over her left thigh both were bouncing like she was working the foot pedal of an old sewing machine. As she did this, she stared at me from behind the Chinese slits that she calls eyes.

She was heated.

I tried to lighten the mood, "Don't you see how hard this dick is?" I grabbed my hard dick and moved it side to side hoping to hypnotize her ass 'til she wasn't mad no more. "You should've had your ass in here naked already, Bae."

She glanced down at my dick, looked back up at me, and rolled her eyes. Then smacked her lips and said, "Please, mister, you can catch blue balls for all I give a damn." She twisted her hair and bounced her legs faster. "Ain't nobody gon be naked in here but you 'til you tell me where the hell you been for the last week."

I looked at her, we stared each other down like two prizefighters in the center of the ring.

A moment later the bell rang.

I took the first swing. "I gotta fight niggas in the streets," I told her. "I don't wanna have to come home and fight you."

She didn't look at me, She just kept on twisting and bouncing. "You ain't been home in how long, mister? And you come back up in here without so much as an explanation? You don't even wanna talk to me? If you think, just 'cause you pay rent up in this bitch, I'm supposed to just let you walk all over me. You must've fell and bumped yo' gotdamn head. My momma ain't raise no fool."

I told her, "Chill out, Princess. Ain't nobody tryna walk all over you. I just wanna leave that street shit in the streets. I don't wanna talk to you about that shit. I'm tryna protect ya ass—"

"Protect me!" she snapped. "Protect me from what, mister? What exactly are you tryna protect me from, huh? You think I don't know you a drug dealer? You don't think I know you in a gang? I know everything you into. I know about the dope in the kitchen cabinet. I know about the gun under the living room sofa. I know about that garbage bag full of weed in yo' closet," she said, then she grabbed my chin and made me look at her. "I know what happened to Fatso. My friend taking that shit hard. I don't know what I would do if a nigga killed you out there in them streets. You ain't protecting me by not talking to me, Dontae. What you doin' is worryin' the shit outta me."

Got damn!

Princess was driving down on me reckless as a muhfucka. But I had to admit it, she did have a point. I would never tell her that, though.

She kept her press on me, "When you asked me if I was ridin' with you till the wheels fall off, and I told you yeah. I meant that shit. But you gotta talk to me, Dontae. You can't keep me in the dark about shit. If you fuckin' other bitches, creepin' on me and shit. Just lemme know—"

"See," I said waggin' a finger at her. "That's yo' problem. You always think a nigga out there trickin' off with other bitches and shit. I ain't got time for that shit. It's a lot goin' on, right now. All I been able to do is think about that shit that happened to Fatso."

"And you bogus, too," Princess said. "You ain't even go to his funeral. Everybody been sayin' how fucked up it was that you didn't pay your last respects, seein' as how tight y'all was."

"Fuck what everybody sayin', Princess," I told her. "I don't give a fuck about what everybody sayin', you shouldn't either. I paid to have my nigga sent off in style. I was at the funeral and the burial. I saw you holdin' Angie while she was fallin' apart."

Princess's eyes popped open at me revealing true events to her.

"I waited till all them fake friends rolled out. I kicked it with my nigga one last time," I told her. "That's what I did. Fuck what everybody else says. All that matters to me is what Ms. Toni and Angie say."

Ms. Toni was Fatso's mother and Angie was his baby momma.

"Now, there it is, Princess," I said grabbing my hard dick. It was throbbin' so bad it hurt. "Now, suck this muhfucka for me or somethin'?"

"Nope, mister, not 'til you tell me where you been and what you been doin' for the past week."

I blew out air and that shit sounded like a blowout tire. Me talking to Princess would be a violation of the Street Nigga Code. A nigga was never supposed to pillow talk with hos. Putting Princess in the street business would definitely be considered pillow talking. But would she fall in the category of hos? After all, she was my main bitch. I had trusted her enough to make her the queen of my castle. I slept around her and kept my ends around her. Why couldn't I talk to her about everything? Princess had me by the balls, literally. Those balls would be blue if I didn't start talking.

"You wanna talk, huh?" I said, frustrated. "You wanna know where I been and what I been doin'. A'ight, here it is."

I told her the stick-up man Reggie Wade had robbed my spot and killed Fatso. I told her I'd gone to Pool Hall and asked him about Reggie Wade, and he told me about his dope addict mother, his treacherous sister Rachel and his serial rapist brother, Ronnie. I told her about Reggie Wade, too, but I left out the ugliest details so she wouldn't be scared. Then I told her about my search for Reggie Wade. My conversation with Streetlight, the room in the Michigan Inn, and how I'd been in the streets in the same clothes, survivin' off weed, liquor, and Ramens. She listened and took all that shit in like a tape recorder.

"If he's as crazy as you say he is, Bae—" Princess said. "—why don't you just get somebody just as crazy as he is to find him and kill him for you?"

I shook my head, leaped up, and started pacing the floor. "I can't do that, Princess. Don't you understand? I gotta handle this shit myself?" I put a hand on my chest. "If I don't the streets gon' lose all respect for me. If I don't find this nigga and buss his shit, I'm gon' lose money. If I lose money, no more comfy, lakefront apartment. No more Gucci bags, Chanel sandals, Louis Vuitton dresses for you. No more BMWs you drive to school. You go back to your mother's crib in Lawless Gardens, and I go back to slangin' dime bags in the stairwell."

I stopped pacing and looked at Princess. She appeared to be processing everything I'd just told her. She twisted her hair and started bouncing her legs again. This time she added the thing she does when she's nervous, she started chewing the inside of her mouth.

When I sat down beside her she stopped twisting, bouncing, and chewing. Then she turned, looked me right in the eye, and said, "Yeah, bae, you need to find that nigga and buss his shit."

I kissed her lips. "I thought you'd see it my way." I leaned over and nibbled her ear. "Now, can I get some pussy? Damn!"

Without a word, Princess scooted back onto the bed. She untied the sash of her robe, opened her legs, and used her fingers to part the juicy flesh between her thighs. Her pink clit popped out of its hood and pulsated like a heartbeat. My dick became even harder. I had to get inside her. I turned over to get on top of her, but before I could, she rocked back and brought her pretty, pedicured feet up to my chest to stop me.

I frowned. "What's up, bae?" I asked. "I thought we kissed and made up?"

She smiled up at me. "We did kiss and makeup, mister. But now you gotta kiss and makeup with Ms. Kitty-Kat. She's still mad at you."

"I gotta kiss and make up with Ms. Kitty-Kat, huh?"

Yeah, mister," she told me. "You had your shower. Now, I'm givin' you yo' pussy and somethin' to eat—in that order."

"I don't know what I'ma do with you."

"You'll figure it out."

She parted her thighs, and I went down on her. I licked and sucked on her wet pussy lips. I kissed her clit and licked circles around it. Then, I sucked it in my mouth, ran my tongue over it, and gave her wet pussy my finger at the same time. I felt her melt under the constant stimulation. She squeezed her plump titties, tweaked her perky nipples, gyrated her hips, and thrust her pelvis forward to meet my tongue. Her salty flesh was soaking wet. Her pussy creamed as she moaned.

"Ummm," she groaned and squirmed. "If you keep your tongue right there—I'm-I'm-I'm gonna—cummmm!" She came trembling and squirting her juices all over my face.

I looked up at her just in time to see her eyes rolling in the back of her head. After a moment she came back from La La-land.

I grinned up at her in triumph. "So," I said as I fingered her wet pussy. "Did Ms. Kitty-Kat forgive me?"

"Ms. Kitty-Kat told me to tell you, she'll give you an answer to that question after you give her Mr. Dick."

After Princess said that, I eased on top of her, and she rocked back to take every inch of me.

Then, she bit down on my neck hard enough to break my skin and said, "You stay away from here another week, mister. And I promise you we gon' throw hands in this muhfucka."

I woke up the following morning with the sun in my face. I'd had the intention to be up and at it last night, but my body had other plans. I'd slept longer than I wanted to. I looked beside me, and Princess was asleep, in the fetal position with a pillow between her knees. We'd gone at it like two jackrabbits for hours on end. I hit the pussy 'til my dick was sore. I knew she was exhausted.

I rolled out of bed, showered, and jumped into a black Nike sweatsuit and Jordan twos. then I walked quietly out of the bedroom, into the kitchen, and set up the glass kitchen table like a science lab. I grabbed the coffee grinder off the kitchen counter, the sifter and waxpaper from one cabinet, and the dope, lactose, a box of sandwich bags, and my digital scale from another cabinet. My other utensils was in the cabinet under the sink. I grabbed those and got down to whippin' up dope.

Princess walked into the kitchen just as I was putting things away.

"You want me to cook you somthin' before you leave, bae?" she asked, as she walked toward me with her robe open, revealing her perky titties and her neatly-shaven pussy.

I told her, "I'm straight, I'll grab something in the streets cause I gotta roll.

She threw her arms around my neck. "You sure?" she asked again. "Cause I can hook you somethin' up real quick." She placed light kisses on my face and grabbed my dick.

I told her, "I know you can, bae, but I gotta go." I kissed her and said, "Leave me somethin' for tonight."

"I got you."

Princess turned and sashayed out of the kitchen with her ass jiggling loosely under her thin silk robe. I almost followed her back to the bedroom, but I couldn't. I had to get to the building and tend to Bomb in a Bag. I needed money to go to war. I pushed the baggie of dope into my pocket and walked out of the kitchen, throwing on my black Marc Bucannan leather. At the door, I pulled my two .40's out and took them off safety. Money wasn't the only thing a nigga needed to go to war. A nigga also needed guns and I had a lot of 'em.

All I did was cut the dope. Cat Eyes and Fatso usually handled all the bagging and distribution, but now that Fatso was gone, one of the young Folks would have to step up. More than likely that would be Sneak. Sneak was hungry, and he would love not having to run the bundles no more. Woo, Lil Mike, and Lil Tonio were up and comin' hustlers, but they were still too young to be focused. Cat Eyes was smart, I knew he'd choose Sneak to take Fatso's spot in the organization.

"Bomb in a Bag! Bomb in a Bag! Bomb in a Bag!" Pool Hall yelled at passing cars as they pulled into the back parking lot of the 534 building. Dope fiends were attacking the building on foot, on bikes and some were even rolling up in wheelchairs.

I pulled into the parking lot just as a caravan of patrol cars went speeding East on 37th Street. That shit spooked me. I had twenty years of prison on me, so I parked quickly, hopped out of The Benz, and ran into the building with the cold wind propelling me forward.

Cat Eyes was in the lobby. He was rocking a cream and green Pelle leather with the matching Wing-Ding hat, jeans, and green-suede, Bally mocassins. He smiled and came toward me.

"You right on time, Folks," he said, walking up on me and hittin' me with the GD handshake, a simple palm slap, and entangling of the index fingers that ended down low with two pitchforks.

After we shook up, I reached into my pocket, pulled out the baggie full of dope, and handed it to Cat Eyes.

Cat Eyes grabbed the baggie, cuffed it, and said, "Jamo and Eddie-Booze just came through this bitch and cleaned us out."

Jamo was the nigga in authority over all the GDs in The Planet Rock area of the projects. He was a slim nigga with a penchant for Argyle clothing and big trucks. Eddie-Booze was a loudmouth hustler who ran neck and neck for the ugliest nigga in the world. All he did was fight dogs and cheat in dice games. Between Jamo, Eddie-Booze, and Iroc Tony I was clearing at least an extra 15,000 dollars a day.

I heard Cat Eyes mention Jamo and Eddie Booze, but I noticed he didn't mention Iroc Tony. So, I asked him, "Iroc Tony ain't come through?"

"That's the shit I was bouta holla at you about," Cat Eyes said as he pulled out a blunt and fired up. "This mornin' muhfuckas got tired of the music blastin' at Iroc Tony's crib. So, they went to the door and found that muhfucka open. When they walked in, he and his bitch was in that muhfucka dead, Folks. A nigga left both of they ass stankin'."

"Lemme guess," I said folding my arms over my chest. "Both of 'em was shot with a shotgun?"

Cat Eyes looked surprised. "How you know?"

He passed me the blunt. I hit it and thought about something Pool Hall had told me.

"But now Iroc Tony gotta be on his P's and Q's cause the boy don't forget or forgive shit. That's one thing about him, bossman—he's all about the even-steven."

While I'd been searching high and low for Reggie Wade, he'd been busy collecting on an old debt. He'd waited five years for revenge, and he'd finally got it.

"Iroc Tony popped the shit outta the nigga Reggie Wade before he went to the joint," I told Cat Eyes as I passed him the blunt.

Cat Eyes hit the blunt and with the smoke in his lungs, and said, "Iroc Tony had to know that nigga was out the joint. I can't believe Folks' ass rocked himself to sleep like that." He shook his head. "After all that time, Folks, that nigga Reggie Wade a piece of work. Why don't you just let me and Sneak get on his bumper?"

"Never that move, Jo'," I said, cutting Cat Eyes off with my hands moving like a baseball umpire calling a runner safe. "I'ma take care of my own business."

"A'ight," Cat Eyes told me, reluctantly. "Take care of yours." He passed me the blunt. "But if shit starts gettin' ugly don't let yo' pride stop you from taggin' the Folks in."

I hit the blunt and told him, "If I need y'all—and that's a big if, I don't know about taggin' y'all in, but I'll definitely take y'all aid and assistance."

Cat Eyes rubbed his palms together, shook up with me again, and said, "And we gon' be there to aid and assist our brotha in all righteous endeavors."

CHAPTER 10
DETECTIVE STEVEN KNOX

The only difference between me and the rest of these lowlife muthafuckas living in these projects is that fresh out of high school, I enlisted in the United States Army, and after receiving an honorable discharge four years later, I came back to this place where I was born and raised on the other side of the law. Now with that said, I don't want you muthafuckas to get this shit misconstrued, just 'cause I'm the police don't mean I believe in the criminal justice system. I ain't out here on no stupid, self-righteous shit, tryna rid the streets of crime. Quite frankly, I believe, as long as it's poor muthafuckas, crime ain't goin' no-damn-where. Crime in this country is a whore everybody gets a chance to sleep with once or twice. So, I ain't no goofy muthafucka running around tryna change the world one arrest at a time. I ain't no dumb ass crime-fighter 'cause the criminal justice system boasts that it would rather free one-hundred guilty men than to convict one innocent man. My system of justice punishes every guilty man, and every now and again, a few innocent muthafuckas catch a bad break. Boo-Fuckin-Hoo, shit happens.

Suck that shit up. I ain't gon' drive myself batshit crazy out here tryna find one grain of brown sugar in a bag of sand. The streets are cruel—especially in the Ida B. Wells Housing Projects. Out here, one of these dope fiend muthafuckas will kill you for money to cop a dime bag. I know some thirteen-year-old killers that'll make John Wayne Gacey and Richard Speck look like tree-hugging flower children. If a law enforcement officer wanna survive out here, he gotta know how to leave that book shit he learned in the classroom and get in the mud with a muthafucka. That's where you will find me—in the mud.

I balance shit out in this bitch. Fuck these ignorant cocksuckers. I will blow one of their ass to smithereens. Jail is for niggas that can be redeemed, a bunch of these muthafuckas don't deserve nothing but killing. It was a cold, windy October day when I bent a left on Ellis Street, and stood on the gas pedal, taking my brown, box Chevy speeding up the one way, to the first building in the Madden Park Homes. I was responding to a call about a double homicide on the 4th floor of the building. I seemed to get all the cases in the projects 'cause I was from here. I knew all the players, all the pimps, whores, and all the pushers. That shit went a long way when most detectives wouldn't set foot in this muthafucka.

The sun was shining but the sunshine did nothing to brighten the day. A dark cloud hung over this bitch like a nuclear plant. The plume over this muthafucka was just as polluted.

As I whipped the steering wheel left and rolled into the parking lot behind the first building, I heard: "Faggot Steve, here, y'all!"

I turned around and spotted a lil' short muthafucka in a nappy, Chicago Bulls skull cap. He was wearing a blue-jean jacket over a black hoodie, blue jeans, and Air Jordan's. He had an overbite that made the smirk on his black ass face appear to be mocking me even more.

I was about to deal with his ass. I had time. The bodies upstairs could wait. It wasn't like they were going anywhere. I jerked the box into park, bailed out, and stormed toward the lil' muthafucka, who had just disrespected me. Jacking my jeans.

"What you call me? You lil' bitch ass nigga!" I growled at the little muthafucka. I looked at him, upped my.357 Magnum and aimed it at his chest. "Go head, bitch. Run. Try me, I'll shoot you in the back and put a gun on you," I said and he froze. "Put your hands up," I told him.

Overbite threw his hands up. I holstered my weapon and gave Overbite a gut punch that made him grunt. In my peripheral, niggas were scattering. I picked Overbite up by the back of his jacket.

Pain was on his face now instead of that smirk I'd seen before.

"You dirty, bitch?" I asked him as I frisked him.

"Nall," he responded, tryna recover from the blow I'd delivered him. "I ain't got shit on me."

"Any needles in yo' pocket, or anything that'll stick me?" I asked.

"Uh-uh."

"Okay, muthafucka," I said in a warnin' tone. "If I put my hands in yo' pocket and some shit sticks me, that's a mouth shot." I searched Overbite and found a pocket full of crumpled bills. I held it in front of him and asked, "Where you get all this bread, bitch?"

"My momma gave it to me," he said.

I looked him in the eye, and he looked at the ground. He was lying. He knew it and I knew it.

I told him, "Do I look like Boo-Boo The Fool to you, bitch? You don't think I know—" I held the money up in his face. "—this right here is dope money. I can smell the crack and Heroin all over it."

I finished searching Overbite and pushed him hard in the chest. He stumbled back a few steps. Then I told him, "Gon' get yo' ass outta here, bitch. And next time I hear you call me Faggot Steve I'ma take you on the train tracks and blow yo' fuckin' brains out. Try me?" I said, then pocketed the wad of cash I found in Overbite's pockets. He didn't walk away. I told him, "Go ahead. Get the fuck outta here, bitch!"

"Gimmie my money back," he challenged.

I struck like a rattle snake, grabbing him by the throat. I put my lips a centimeter from his ear as he choked. "What money, bitch?" I growled. "Whose money is this?"

"It's yours." He gurgled again.

I let go of my grip on his neck, he bent over coughing.

I told him, "Get your dope dealin' ass outta here before I fuck you up." I then turned and walked back toward the first building.

A couple of bodies was waiting for me upstairs. I had kept them waiting too long.

Apartment 406.

The air in the small apartment smelled like death. If you want to know what death smells like, it smells like shit, piss, coagulated blood, and gasoline. I walked by bluecoats in the hallway, and when I made it to the living room I found Jill Marie Brown the 48th District's number one Crime Scene Investigator standing over two white sheets. Two bodies were etched out under the sheets. Blotches of blood had seeped through them, and parts of them could be cut out and used as a Japanese flag.

I looked at Jill. She was plain-Jane, but she was pretty in a Claire Huxtable kinda way. I'd always wanted to fuck Claire Huxtable.

I asked, "What we got here?"

She looked up from her memo pad and said, "Black male, black female victims. Single gunshot wounds to the head. Bound and tied. Looks like a robbery-homicide."

I squatted on my haunches beside the bodies.

"If you're gonna take a look, Steven," Jill said. "I hope you haven't had breakfast." She handed me a pair of rubber gloves.

I took them and snapped them on. "Is it that bad?"

She said, "See for yourself?"

I did just that. When I pulled the sheets back, I saw a gruesome sight. Half of the victim's heads were gone, and in place of them was a mixture of skull and brain fragments, bone and blood. The ghastly mixture resembled elbow noodles in thick tomato soup.

"They made a positive I.D.?" I asked as I scrutinized the bodies.

"Anthony Shields and Nicole Leigh Daniels," she told me. "You know 'em?"

"I know Anthony Shields," I told her. "Iroc Tony." I looked over Iroc Tony's wounds.

"Somebody fucked you up royally, Mr. Dope man. And you got yo' girlfriend here fucked up royally, too. Who the fuck did you piss off?" I mumbled.

From the looks of it, both victims had been shot with a shotgun. Which wouldn't've meant shit to me if I hadn't just started working another case over in the 534 building where another dope dealer who went by the name Fatso had been shot with a shotgun. I looked down on the floor around the bodies and spotted a bunch of little zip loc bags with bomb logos on 'em. The little zip loc bags was the same empty bags I'd found discarded in the lobby of the 534 building. They belonged to Bomb in a Bag, a Heroin brand ran by Baby Don's son, Dontae Kirkpatrick. It didn't take a rocket science to figure out that somebody was robbing and killing Dontae's people. Whoever it was, was doing his work with a shotgun. There was only one nigga that worked a shotgun with this much surgical precision, and I'd sent his ass to prison five years ago.

I stood up and waved a bluecoat over, a white boy with a potbelly.

He came over to me.

I placed a hand on his shoulder and told him, "I want you to run a name for me."

The bluecoat pulled out a pen and pad, held it inches from his pad, and asked, "What's the name, sir?"

I told him, "Reginald...Bernard...Wade!"

CHAPTER 11

DONTAE

I got up on 39th and Vincennes just as the sun came out, but it was still cold and windy. Even so, the I&L Liquor Store parking lot was jam-packed. Dope fiends stood in the parking lot all day, yelling dope names at passing cars. When the cars stopped, the dope fiends hopped in and took them to the dope lines in the projects. The dope fiends at the I&L Liquor Store were called *runners*, and the more they saw at the dope line, the more they were paid. So, they did their jobs with serious pride.

The dilapidated storefronts running up and down 39th Street, from State to the Lake was full of these runners. Also, in their mix was a gang of street vendors, wine heads, and panhandlers.

By 9:00 a.m. 39th Street resembled an open-air flea market for dope.

"Thunder!" one of the runners shouted.

"Famous!" another runner shouted.

"Twenty Paid!" another runner shouted.

I pulled into the parking lot and looked around. The crowds were out of control. The competition was heated.

I rolled down my window.

"Thunder got a bomb today, Mack Buddy!" one of the runners yelled into a beat-up Oldsmobile.

Pool Hall came walking out of the store with a brown paper bag. "Bomb in a Bag!" he yelled as he pulled the bag down off the neck of his wine bottle and made a shirt for it. "Bomb on the white! You pass us by, and you won't get high!" he said, then spotted me and walked over to the car.

He was wearing a black Kangol over his nappy afro, a blue jean jacket, burgundy sweats, and an old, hand-me-down pair of British Knights that Fatso probably blessed him with. A wet toothpick dangled from his pink lips.

"Bossman," Pool Hall said as he stood beside my driver's window. "Early bird gets the worm. And we up and at em today."

I asked him, "How that thang is?" I was asking about the potency of the dope I'd put out this morning.

"I got an instant rush," he said, rocking a little and sucking his teeth. "I'll tell you 'round lunch if it got legs."

"Yeah, you do that," I told him as I looked around.

I was looking for Dirty Bird. The Canons usually came through the I&L parking lot every morning before they went to work. Going to work for them was heading downtown to pick pockets, play checks and credit cards, boost, or all of the above. The Canons that snorted dope liked to get high before they played their games, and this was where they usually came to get their blows.

"You seen, Dirty Bird, old nigga?"

Pool Hall took a swig of his wine. "Uh-uh, not this mornin'. Glo' came through, though. That's his broad Cross Country over there," Pool Hall told me, pointing a fat finger at Cross Country.

The nigga Cross Country was standing not ten feet away, slender, and thin-shouldered in a beige trench coat and a beige Fedora with a blue feather. The creases up the front of his brown slacks could dice vegetables. His brown, suede loafers didn't have a speck of dirt on 'em. Cross Country was one of the coldest Canons to play the game. Rumor had it that he'd played last year's Mardi Gras and tore that shit up for 250,000 dollars. That was the rumor, I didn't know how true it was.

"Ask him if he seen him. They be workin' together sometimes," Pool Hall said.

I stepped on the gas and pulled beside Cross Country. "Cee-Cee, check it out, Jo'." I waved him over. "Lemme holla at you."

Cross Country walked closer to the Benz, admiring it. "What's up, shorty?" he said with a smile. "I see you ridin' real slick."

"This ain't shit," I told him, dismissing his compliment.

Compliments out here wasn't worth the breath used to give 'em. They almost always came before some kinda grift.

"But aye...I was wonderin' if you seen Dirty Bird?"

Cross Country pulled out a cigarette and fired up. "Dirty Bird popped, Jo," he said.

"Straight up?" I asked, surprised.

"And down," Cross Country countered. "He saw a mog sleep walking outta the Hancock building and got dead on his bumper, no stick, no shade. A Samaritan got all in his smitty. The vic fan and the twist snatch him up. When he beat the mog for his stain, the mog tells the twist he bumped him, so he sittin' for a strong-armed instead-a theft. That's buzzard luck," Cross Country said, shaking his head.

I shook mine, too. For no reason other than I was looking for Dirty Bird so he could help me track down Reggie Wade. From what Cross Country had just explained, Dirty Bird had got popped by the law tryna pick a nigga's pockets downtown. I was the one with the buzzard luck.

I was ready to pull off, but Cross Country stopped me. "You fuck with that jay, shorty?" he asked, referring to if I bought jewelry in the streets.

"Yeah, I fuck with it," I told him. "As long as that shit ain't no slum."

Cross Country turned his nose up like I assassinated his character. "I'ma wiz, shorty, I don't fuck around wit' slum jay. I'm finna put together a few lids. My bitch a writer, we gon' play for the lil merch," he said, then thumped his cigarette to the ground and asked, "Where you posted up at?"

I told him, "The five-thirty-four buildin'."

"Oh," he said. "You in the body bag buildings, Huh? Bomb in a Bag," he mumbled the Bomb in a Bag part of his statement almost as if he was talking to himself. Then, he told me, "I'ma go to work, then I'ma bend back on you later, Jo'."

I told him, "I ain't gon' hold my breath."

He told me, "My word gold, shorty."

I threw the Benz in drive.

Cross County sat his forearms on the frame of the driver's window. "Shorty?"

I said, "What's up?"

He said, "I heard y'all got a bomb over there today. I'm ill. Get me out the gate and I swear one hand gon' wash the other."

I looked at Cross Country for a moment, the shame in his eyes told me he was just a hustler down on his luck. The rumors about the $250,000 stain couldn't have been true. If it was, that means the nigga had blown through a quarter-million dollars. If he'd did that, he wasn't much of a hustler at all. I was finna see if he was a man of his word.

I told him, "Hop in, I'll drive you over there."

After dropping Cross Country off at the building, I headed for the Lakegrove apartment complex. Princess had told me how hard Angie was taking Fatso's death, so I knew I had to come check on her. Fatso's three-year-old son Rashaun and his baby momma Angie was my responsibility now. It was the least I could do for my fallen comrade.

I parked the Benz, hopped out, and walked into Angie's building. I pushed the buzzer to her apartment and waited. A second later she answered. I said my name and the glass door beside me clicked and buzzed like an old typewriter. I walked through the door, caught the elevator to the 8th floor, and walked down a hallway with doors on both sides. Angie lives in apartment, 805. When I got to the door, it was open.

I walked in and it clicked closed behind me.

The TV was on, a re-run of *What's Happenin'* was playin'. I walked into the living room and found Angie on the couch. A wine bottle was on the table, joint roaches in the ashtray, and the air smelled like Skunk weed. I looked at Angie. She was a little thing with a slanted bob and maroon highlights that went good with her red-bone complexion.

She was petite and cute, her eyes were pink and puffy from crying and smoking weed. Even in an oversized T-shirt and pajama pants, even in the shape, she was in, she still looked good. Fatso had a pretty baby momma.

"Hey, Dontae," Angie said, barely audible.

"Hey, sis," I said, walking further into the living room.

She looked up at me and saw the dark circles forming under her eyes. She hadn't had much sleep since Fatso's death. Me either.

She said, "Ms. Toni told me what you did, too. That was some real shit. She didn't have no insurance on Fatso. She would've never been able to do that funeral without you."

A couple of days after Fatso was killed, I had stopped in on Ms. Toni and gave her $10,000. I hadn't said anything to anybody 'cause I wasn't looking for a pat on the back.

"That shit wasn't nothin', sis," I told her. "But how you and Rashaun been?"

She sniffled a little and held back tears. "Dontae," she said. "I miss Fatso. I haven't even washed our sheets 'cause I can still smell him in 'em. I still see him. I'll turn around after hearin' him call my name, and he'll be standin' there. I reach out for him in the middle of the night. And when I touch the cold sheets, I remember he's dead and I cry myself back to sleep. Rashaun wakes up every mornin' askin' me where his daddy is, Dontae. I know he saw him in the casket, but he thinks Fatso was just asleep. How am I supposed to tell my three-year-old son that his daddy is dead and he's never comin' back?" She looked my way for an answer.

I didn't have one for her. I was struggling to make sense of all this shit myself.

Angie broke down, she put her face in her palms and cried from her soul. I took a seat beside her and threw an arm around.

I rubbed circles on her back and told her, "Everything's gon' be a'ight. You'll get over it and get on with your life. Time will heal yo' broken heart." I told her all of this as she cried in my chest 'til the front of my hoodie was wet.

Angie was in pain, and her pain was inconsolable. Hers was pain of a young mother that had just suffered the tragic loss of her child's father to the streets. I held Angie as she released her pain... pain that needed to be released.

I knew this 'cause it was my unreleased pain that fed the monster inside of me.

Angie sobbed into my chest for what, to me felt like hours.

What's Happenin' went off the TV, the credits rolled, and after that *Good Times* came on.

Angie was still in my chest crying when Good Times went off. She was in a dark place, a place some muhfuckas didn't come back from.

I had to help her.

I told her, "Angie, pull yourself together. Fatso wouldn't want you to be fallin' apart over him like this. You gotta be strong. Not just for you, but for Rashaun."

She sat up slowly and nodded. "You're right, Dontae," she cried. "You're right, I need to get it together."

I grabbed her face, she closed her eyes and I used my thumb to wipe away her tears. Then, we separated, I rolled a joint and fired it up.

She told me, "Princess left that shit here."

I told her, "I figured that."

Angie smiled, even though I knew smiling was hard for her. I smiled back and passed her the joint.

She hit the joint and said, "Fatso loved and admired you, Dontae." That made me feel good. Angie continued, "All he did was talk about you. Right before he got killed, he told me you was gon' okay his own spot and when you did, he was gon' buy him a Benz just like yours."

"He told you that, huh?" I see I'm not the only one pillow talkin'.

"Yup." Angie nodded and passed me the joint. "I mean it. He talked about you all the time."

Tears welled in her eyes and she sucked her bottom lip in under her top row of teeth.

I put the joint out. Then reached in my pocket, pulled out a wad of cash, and handed it to her. "That's for you and Rashaun, sis. If you need anything else, I mean anything don't hesitate to ask."

She slid the wad of cash under the sofa pillow. "Thanks, Dontae," she told me with soft eyes. "Thanks for everything."

"I ain't doin' nothin' Fatso wouldn't have done for me," I told her, then stood up. "I gotta be up, sis."

She stood up. "I'll walk you out."

She followed me to the door, "Dontae," she said. "Don't let that nigga get away with that shit."

I told her, "Don't worry, sis. That nigga livin' on borrowed time."

I gave her a hug, kissed her tear, wet cheek, and for an awkward moment, her big brown eyes gazed into mine like she needed me in a way that we both knew wasn't right.

I let her go.

She let me go.

We let the moment go.

Then, I turned and walked out of the apartment confused about what had just occurred between me and Angie.

Downstairs, I ran into Ms. Toni.

Fatso's old G was a thick woman with peanut butter skin and blond dreadlocks. She was wearing a wool, Kente print smock over a black turtleneck sweater, and her jeans were tight down to her black riding boots with the three-inch heels.

Ms. Toni was forty years old, but she was the kind of forty that would have a young nigga chasing her ass.

"You just left Angie's?" she asked, adjusting her Kente print purse on her forearm.

I told her, "Yeah, I was up there checkin' on her."

"How is she?"

"You need to sit with her for a while."

I looked at Ms. Toni. She had gone through her sad phase. Her sadness was now anger. She asked me, "Dontae, that nigga that killed my baby still walkin' around here?"

I told her, "Not for long, Ms. Toni."

She tapped me on my shoulder. "Good," she said. "Cause, my heart gon' be heavy till I hear that nigga's dead. He shouldn't get to walk around and my son gotta lay cold in the ground."

"You're right, Ms. Toni. I got that nigga," I told her. "When he sees me, my face gon' be the last face he sees."

CHAPTER 12
CAT EYES

A dope fiend who went by Congo walked up on the building just as the sun was going down.

I was standing on the stairs, noticing that traffic had slowed down since earlier. Congo came toward me. He was wearing a wool cap and a navy peacoat. A full-length, white garb flowed down to his boots. A leather strap held an African drum on his back. Congo got his ends and came to Bomb in a Bag every night. As he got closer I saw the tired look on his face. I asked him to play me a song.

"I would, Catman," he told me showing me his hands. "But my hands, I gotta give' em a rest."

They looked like, if they were chopped off, they'd hit the ground, get up on the fingers and take off running. The palms of his hands were calloused to the point where a six-inch husk had grown on 'em. The lifelines looked like rivers of blood. Congo's hands were fucked up.

I told him, "Yours on me tonight, Congo," I said, then peeled and gave him a dub. "You just make sure you come back another time and play somethin' for me."

Congo smiled. "I got you, Catman."

He ran off to the building happy as fag in dick land.

He wasn't gone long before he came back with a salty look on his face. Showing me the bag he'd bought with my dub.

"Catman," he said, givin' me the bag. "This how y'all thang comin' tonight?"

I took a nice, hard look at the bag, it had the Bomb in a Bag logos on it, but from the skimpy size of it and the smeared look around the zip seal, I could tell the bag had been dipped into.

My lips curled as I pulled out another dub and gave it to Congo.

I told him, "Go buy another bag, and bring it back to me, Congo."

Congo took off and I waited in front of the building for him to come back. He came back with another bag that had been dipped in. Suddenly, I realized why our traffic had slowed down. Whoever was pitching the bundles today was dropping in the bags.

I told Congo, "You go ahead and keep these." I handed him the dipped-in bags. "When you come back through tomorrow the bags be straight."

"Yeah, Catman," Congo said with his nose turned up. "That lousy nigga up there is bad for business."

I walked into the building as Congo walked away. Sneak, Lil Mike, Lil 'Tonio, and Woo was in the lobby. I asked Woo who was pitching since he was running the bundles to the pitcher today.

Woo's lil' bird face ass looked at me and asked, "Why, Gee, what's up?"

I told him, "Whoever it is, is dippin' in the bags. And that shit comin' out yo' pay."

"Why the fuck it gotta come outta my pay?" Woo protested.

I told him, "Cause the pitcher is yo' responsibility. You lil' small-time, street punk. Everybody gotta job to do out here, and I expect a muhfucka to do yours."

Sneak tugged his black Wing-Ding down lower on his forehead and told me, "That nigga House been pitchin' today."

I curled my lips and nodded. House was a known shiester, a little skinny nigga who smoked crack out of the can. Whoever had hired him was definitely sweet.

I told Sneak, "Take these three stupid muhfuckas up there and deal with House's ass thoroughly. I'll be up there after I tell the customer we'll be back on in ten minutes."

By the time I made it up to the 2nd floor of the building, I heard screaming coming from a vaco a couple of doors down from the stairwell. I pushed the door of the vaco, walked in, and found Sneak standing there smoking a blunt as Woo, Lil' Mike and Lil' Tonio beat the dog shit outta House. They'd stripped him ass naked and it looked like they'd snatched the 2 by 4s they were beating House with, off the boards Public Housing had nailed over the vaco windows cause they still had the nails in 'em.

House screamed like he was burning up in a fire as Woo, Lil' Mike and Lil' Tonio raised the spiked 2 by 4s and brought 'em down on every part of his body, repeatedly and savagely. Every so often, the nails got stuck, and the young niggas would have to hold House in place with a foot on his neck, to snatch the 2 by 4s back. Whenever that happened, blood would leap outta him and splatter the walls. The beating went on like this until it looked like the young niggas was pummeling a side of bloody beef. The floor and the walls were covered in thick, red blood.

I told my young niggas, "Now, take his ass to the incinerator with the rest of the trash."

I stood aside as my young niggas picked House's almost lifeless body up by his hands and feet and carried him out of the vaco. Me and Sneak followed them up the dark hallway, down to the incinerator.

Sneak opened the iron, incinerator door and Lil' Mike and Lil' Tonio stuffed House inside. When he slid down the fiery, chute, Woo slammed the iron door shut.

You had to be brutal out here in these streets. Niggas had to know if they fucked up, they got fucked up.

CHAPTER 13
REGGIE WADE

The Darrow Homes section of *The Wells* was nothing but four, 14-story buildings the color of a rotten pumpkin. Dark porches shot up the front of the buildings behind mesh fencing. Every so often shadows zig-zagged through breezeways, the kinda shadows that could leap out and blow a nigga's brains out. It was late when I fought the hawk across Langley at 38th Street, and walked into the dark bowels of the 727 building.

I saw no one, but I knew that didn't mean no one saw me. I felt Iroc Tony's Desert Eagles against ribs. My hands were wrapped around the duct tape handle of The Beast. This made me feel better about entering a building that was known for not letting niggas out alive. In the dimly lit stairwell, I heard music throbbing the *West Coast* gangsta rapper AMG was rapping *Bitch Better Have My Money*. I climbed what seemed like never-ending stairs.

Low muttering caught my attention. Then I saw a young nigga pass a female something. After that, she sank to her knees, unbuckled him, unzipped him, whipped his dick out, and started suckin' it.

I saw that shit and didn't. On the 6th Floor, I walked out of the stairwell, onto the porch. Somebody was frying onions and sausages.

My stomach growled. Ignored it and kept walking up the porch to apartment 602, my old running buddy Sky's crib. Apartment 602. I had spent many nights inside this crib high as a lab rat. Me and Sky would retreat here after a good stain and hold up for days on end. I hoped he still lived here.

Knock! Knock! Knock!

I rapped on the wooden door hard, which sent a stinging sensation through my hand. I waited for an answer. When I didn't get one, I laid hard on the door again with my knuckles.

Knock! Knock!

The hollow door on my boney knuckles gave off a nice echo. I stood outside the door for two minutes that felt like a temporary forever. I was about to turn and walk away when I finally heard shoes shuffling to the door. I looked at the window beside it. A sheer curtain moved aside, and two golf ball-sized eyes peeped out from that space and touched me, the porch, and everything else.

A raspy voice came through the door. "That you R-W?"

"Yeah, it's me muhfucka!" I shouted. "Now, stop tweaking and geeking and open this fucking door, vic. It's cold as polar bear's pussy out here."

Locks click-clacked and the door swung into the apartment.

"Well, I'll be got damn!"

I looked over the nigga in front of me. It was Sky but it wasn't the Sky I remembered. This Sky had a hole in his nappy, natural skin, blotchy with rashes, limbs thin as naked tree branches. His boney frame was covered in an old knit sweater that swallowed him whole, and he was wearing the dirtiest, holiest jeans I'd ever seen.

Only the crack pipe was capable of making a nigga neglect himself like this.

Sky had hit rock bottom.

I stood there stuck as Sky continued, "R-W, you don' finally made it home, huh?" he said, then smiled, his crusty ass lips cracked and bled from three different places. "Well...don't just stand there. Understand me? Bring yo' ass in here goofy mog."

I let him pull me into his thin hug. It felt like I was walking through bushes. I didn't hug him back for fear I'd break his scrawny ass.

He let me go.

I walked into the crib and he locked up behind me.

I checked the joint out, I had been in some shitholes, but this one was a fucking trash heap. The living room was fully furnished with shit you'd see on the sidewalk after a muhfucka got evicted. The kitchen was filthy. Roaches congregated on the counter tops, the walls, the floor, and the sink, where a mountain of dirty dishes sat in water that smelled like a backed-up sewer.

The flimsy kitchen table was covered with empty crack bags, broken cigarette lighters, pieces of steel wool, and generic beer cans with holes on the side. Had Sky been anybody else, I would've found somewhere else to get high.

I sat down in a weak chair across from him. I was careful about sitting cause I thought the chair wouldn't hold me, but it did. I took another look at Sky. His left eye was still cocked like a Revolver.

I asked him, "What you been up to, Sky?"

He shrugged. "Nathan, R-W, understand me?" he said. "Everything been down. You ain't gotta ack like you can't tell."

Sky was in bad shape and he knew it. No sense in fronting with him.

"Shit, Sky," I told him. "You down bad as a muhfucka."

"Yeah, R-W. Understand me? The crack got me."

It was so hard for me to understand how one of the most successful stick-up men on the Low end had hit the ground.

I asked, "What happened to you, Sky?"

"I took all them bullets from Stretcher, understand me?" Sky said. "I ain't been back since, R-W. The nigga put me out commission."

My eyebrows met in the middle of my head. I had heard Stretcher another member of our old Dirty Snatcher's gang, had shot Sky eleven times. The cold part about it was Doreen Pitts a broad Sky had beat outta some scratch, had made the ambulance call. A nigga never knew who he might need in this world.

I told him, "You down now, but you definitely ain't out vic. One thing for sure and two things for certain. You been down before, so you know how to get back up."

He threw a hand at me. "My stick-up days is over, R-W. Understand me?" he said, adjusting himself in his chair. "Stick-up men ain't got a long career out here no more. Understand me? I don' hung up my gloves and sold my pistols for crack, R-W. The stick-up game over with in these here projects, R-W. Understand me?"

He finished talking and picked up the beer can closest to him. Then he picked up a yellow Bic lighter that was missing the metal guard rail on its top. After that, he held the mouth of the can to his crusty lips, held the lighter to the hole in the side of the can, and sparked it. The flame damned near licked the ceiling. What he did next floored me. As the crack sizzled on the can, he sucked the mouth of it hard enough to siphon gas through a rubber hose from the tank of a car.

He did this for a while. Then he sat the can and lighter back on the table and held the smoke in his lungs so long I thought the nigga would pass the fuck out. Finally, his neck loosened, and his head fell back like the top of a Pez candy dispenser. At the same time, he opened his mouth wide enough to yawn and blew out a fragrant fog that turned the whole kitchen hazy. I thought I had seen it all 'till Sky sat there in his chair, still as a stop sign, left eye twitching, lips moving like he wanted to talk, but couldn't. If I hadn't seen it with my own eyes, I wouldn't've believed it. It was officially my main man fifty grand was smoking crack out of the can.

Suddenly, the nigga stood to his feet and went searching the floor for shit.

I snapped, "Sky, sit yo' geekin' ass back down, vic!"

It took him a couple of tries, but he sat his narrow ass back down in his chair.

I waited a while for him to come back to Earth. When he finally landed, I reached into the pocket of my trench coat, pulled out a bundle of dope, and tossed it on the table. "If the stick-up game's over with in these projects—" I said. "—then how the fuck did I come up on this, vic?"

Sky's good eye looked down at the bundle of dope. He picked it up and turned it over in his hands a few times examining it. Then suddenly, he tossed it like burning hot coal back across the table to me.

I glared at him like he'd lost his fucking mind. "Go 'head, vic. You need to get some of that shit up in you," I told him. "Maybe then you'd bring yo' ass off the Starship Enterprise."

He shook his head fast enough to tear it off his neck. "No, R-W," he said.

I would have been a damn fool if I didn't see the fear in his eyes as he stubbornly denied my offer.

"Get that shit outta here. I don't want no parts of that shit. Understand me?"

At first, I thought he was paranoid cause of the crack he'd just smoked. But then I looked into his eyes and saw something else. Something like the look niggas gave me when I stuck The Beast in their faces. I picked the bundle up, opened it, and laid a few bags out on the table.

"What the fuck is wrong with you? You still toot dope, right, vic?" I asked. "This dope is good dope, too."

"I still toot dope, R-W. Understand me?" he said. "But that ain't just any ole' dope. That dope came from Bomb in Bag."

I held a nostril and snorted a line with the other. "The shit is a nuke, too, vic."

"R-W," he said in a low voice. "Tell me you didn't stick-up Bomb in a Bag?"

I felt a grimace tighten on my face. "Yeah, vic, I stuck up Bomb in a Bag. And?" I growled.

Sky was starting to piss me off with this ho shit. I wanted to slap the shit outta his crackhead ass. When did he start riding nigga's dicks?

"Bomb in a Bag is them Lil' GDs dope, R-W," he explained. "They asses been out here killin' like a muhfucka since you been gone. Understand me? You need to listen to me, R-W. Everything don' changed in these projects. Us Dirty Snatcher Disciples is the last of a dyin' breed. A few years back, all the lil' shorties dropped them old slogans and came together as one."

I fired up a square. "Yeah, vic," I challenged. "And what's yo' point?"

"After they came together, they started spray paintin' *GD or Die* everywhere and killin' old niggas that like takin' money," Sky said, then leaned in on the table and started talking with his hands. "Member, Ski-Wee?"

"Yeah, vic, Ski-Wee was my nigga." I treated my nose again.

Sky fired up a square.

I couldn't help but notice he was trembling.

"Them shorties caught him and tossed him in the trunk of a car," he said. "Then they threw in a lit stick of dynamite. The shit exploded and blew Ski-Wee's ass to pieces." Sky frowned and shook his head. "They don't play fair, R-W. Understand me?" He smashed his square out right on the table. "They don't play fair."

I smashed my square out on the table, too. Then I busted down a few more bags of dope and said, "Ski-Wee got caught snoozin', Sky. You know when you snooze you lose."

"See, R-W," he protested. "There you go with that ole bullheaded shit. Understand me? Them shorties is some brutal lil' muhfuckas. You ain't heard about what they did to Big Dingas?"

I snorted a line. "Nall," I said as I pinched my nose. "What happened to Big Dingas?"

"They stood over him with AK-47s and shot him twenty-nine times," he whined like a bitch.

I wanted to tell him to grow a pair of nuts, but I realized he had been castrated a long time ago.

He continued, "They was so close up on him the shots made his clothes catch fire. His body burned to a crisp right up there in the middle of thirty-ninth Street, R-W. Understand me?"

I listened to Sky as he tried to scare me straight, but he still hadn't convinced me the stick-up game was over in the projects. What he had managed to convince of was the stick-up game was over for him.

"Mongo, P.V., Reese-Sco. All dead in the five years you been gone," Sky said, then fired up another square. His hands were trembling so bad he could hardly touch the lighter's flame to the tip of his cancer stick. "All them niggas was out here stickin' up them lil 'GDs, and them lil reckless muhfuckas turned they switch off. Them lil Bomb in a Bag muhfuckas in the Body Bag Buildings is the worst."

I was listening closely now, I knew Sky was about to say some shit I needed to hear.

"Dontae is the alpha in that wolf pack. He supplies all that Bomb in a Bag shit. He runs the five-thirty-four building, too. And every nigga that don' fucked with him, don' got an example made outta his ass. Understand me? They got a sayin'—ain't no—"

"One man, bigga' than the mob," I cut him off.

"You heard that shit before, huh?"

"Yeah," I replied with a slow nod. "They say that shit in the joint, too. But that shit don't put no fear in my heart," I said, then snorted more dope. I was feeling like the toughest, angriest nigga in the world now. "Fuck them puss' ass GDs, Sky. I ain't barrin' none. They can all eat my dick. As far as I'm concerned, every nigga's a gangsta till they meet a real one, vic. And I'm oh-so-for real. Reggie Wade back in the muhfuckin' streets. Niggas better be good or be good at poppin' that thang. Cause I take shit. That's what the fuck I do. You make it, I take it. And ain't a nigga in this world gon' stop me. Muhfuckas want my head, he can't leave his shit at home. Back in the days—"

"There you go with that back in the days shit," Sky snapped. "This ain't back in the days, R-W. Understand me?" He brought a boney fist down on the table that hardly made a sound. "You gon' get yo' fool ass killed and a lotta other muhfuckas out here fuckin' with these shorties. Understand me? They got the numbers—"

It was my turn to bring a fist down on the table. I almost broke the raggedy muhfucka. "Fuck they numbers, Sky!" I shouted. "Bitch ass niggas draw off numbers. I'm cut from a different cloth. You know that shit, vic. I'm built the other kind of way. Ain't no bend, break, or fold in me. I play for keeps! I'll sleep in a nigga's hallway, I'll sleep under a nigga car, I'll creep through a nigga's window. Muhfuckas can run up if he want to. I'ma give a nigga everything he's lookin' for."

Sky snarled at me, "A'ight, Mr. Tough Ass."

"I ain't Mr. Tough Ass, but Mr. Tough Ass ain't gon' fuck with me," I spat. "I do this shit for a reason, not a season, vic. My hustle got meanin' out here in these streets. This shit is spiritual to me. If I catch a nigga servin' while them shorties gettin' outta school. I'm on his ass. If a nigga like jumpin' on muhfuckas that get high, I'm on his ass. If his bitch ass lied to God and said he was just gon' hustle for six months just to get on his feet, and he in the game a day pass six months, I'm on his muhfuckin' ass. Straight like that!"

Sky chuckled. "Same ole R-W," Sky said. "Head like a brick."

"I don't know how to be nobody else but me, vic."

Sky smashed another square out on the table.

I did, too.

He hit some dope with me. Then he told me, "I see you got your mind made up about this shit. Understand me? All I gotta say is, be careful."

"Nall, vic," I told him. "You be helpful and tell me who the fuck is Dontae?" I said, then threw my right leg over my left. "Cause I keep hearin' his name like he's King David 'round this bitch."

Sky nodded. "He the closest thing to King David 'round here," he said, with the whole dick in his ass now. "Dontae is the nigga Baby Don's son. You remember Baby Don and Joyce, right?"

I thought about the flamboyant hustler from the Body Bag Building. He ran the streets back when Billie Harris, Michael Bell, and Baby Head was rolling. Those people found him shot the fuck up in his brand new, white Excaliber with all his jewelry on and his bankroll still in his pocket. The rumor was he'd took off on some Diagos from out in Cicero and got away with some major paper.

That was the rumor. His bitch Joyce was one of the finest red bones in the city.

I told Sky, "Yeah, I remember Baby Don and Joyce."

"Well—like father, like son. Understand me?" Sky said. "The boy's smooth, but still got that ice runnin' through his veins. He don' caught a body every year since you been gone. He ain't one of them leaders that surround himself with a bunch of send-off men. He pops that thang, too. Don't sleep on him. Understand me? Take him seriously. You'll pay for it if you don't. Youngin' got some play for keeps with him."

I smoked that shit over for a hard moment. I had been right to keep Dontae on my mind. Now that I'd finally heard the young nigga's resume and his pedigree, I understood why fat boy had been so sure he'd be on my ass. Dontae wasn't for none, he was a killer. If he moved anything like his old man in his heyday, he was a killer you wouldn't see coming till it was too late.

Attentively, I questioned Sky, taking note of every minor detail he gave me about Dontae. He told me Dontae drove a black Benz 190 with dark tints and chrome AMG rims, but he could be in any other kind of car cause his resources were unlimited. He told me he had khaki-colored skin and wore his hair in two, velvet-sized rope braids. He wasn't tall, or short, and he wasn't stocky or was he skinny. According to what Sky told me, he wasn't one of those reckless young niggas who couldn't think pass go. He didn't do senseless shit and when he murked a nigga, he murked a nigga for a reason.

I listened to Sky as he gave me the complete rundown on Dontae. I had to admit, the young nigga sounded impressive. Still, I loved my chances against any nigga in the streets. So, at the end of the day, I looked at Sky like he was giving the young muhfucka too much credit. After all, Dontae was just now earning his name in the streets. While my name was all through this bitch etched in stone. In the past, I had been the cause of many mothers sitting on the front pew, in all black, crying. I had been the cause of plenty of murals, vigils, and memorials.

If Dontae thought he could spook me out of the streets, he had another thing coming. I smashed a square out on the table, uncrossed my legs, and stood to my feet. I held onto the table until my world stopped spinning. After that, I grabbed the bundle off the table, tucked it, and asked Sky if he had seen the bitch Streetlight.

Sky chuckled. "You still sweet on that trick ass ho', huh?"

My face had no give. "Somethin' like that, vic," I said. "You seen her?"

"Not lately, R-W. Understand me?" he said. "But her funky ass lives over there in the complex on thirty-sixth and Indiana."

I made a mental note and headed for the door. "I'ma holla at you later, vic."

"Come through anytime, R-W."

I got to the door and opened it. Before I made it out onto the porch, Sky held up a crooked finger and said, "Ho!" Then turned and jetted back inside the kitchen. He returned a second later and pushed the empty Bomb in a Bag dope bag into my chest. "Take these with you, R-W. Understand me? That way if they come by here lookin' for you, I can tell 'em I ain't seen yo' ass."

I wasn't even all the way out of the door before he closed it and locked me out. Ain't that a bitch. Smokin' that crack out a can had turned my main man into a coldblooded ho'.

I turned away from the door, and an eerie feeling came over me. It made the hair on the back of my neck stand up. I felt like I was being watched. I looked to the right. Then to the left and saw a silhouette at the end of the porch. It stood there for an odd moment and sold me death on an ice-cold breeze. I swung The Beast upward. That chased the silhouette further into the darkness. I thought about chasing after it but quickly decided against that thought. There was a certain woman I needed to see. I was on my way to 36th and Indiana.

CHAPTER 14
DONTAE

"On the G, Folks. I saw the same nigga that shot Fatso comin' outta this crib."

That was Sneak, he was standing on the fact that he'd spotted Reggie Wade walking out of apartment 602. Sneak was standing there in an all-black sweatsuit, hoodie tight on his braids, stacking his two fists right over left, which was the way we GDs demonstrated we were telling the truth. Passionately, he started explaining that he'd been creeping with a young bitch from the 727 building when he saw Reggie Wade. He said the nigga had peeped him on his bumper and upped a double-barrel shotgun.

Afterward, he'd got to a horn and hit me and Cat Eyes up. However, by the time me and Cat Eyes got to the 727 building the nigga, Reggie Wade was gone. As soon as I realized we'd lost Reggie Wade anger motivated me to lead Cat Eyes and Sneak up to apartment 602, where we kicked the door in and found an old crackhead nigga inside, smoking rocks out of a can.

"Where the fuck Reggie Wade go?" I growled at him.

"Wh-wh-who?" the old nigga stuttered.

Cat Eyes and Sneak started bucking the mog. They scraped him 'till his head resembled a jack-o-lantern. I tossed the place while they were busy giving the old crackhead a pumpkin head. All I heard was gym shoes scuffing the floor, flesh being pounded, and grunts coming from the gut. I was in the old nigga's bedroom, which was nothing but a small area with a busted mattress and a box-spring in a corner beside a black and white 13-inch television sitting on a red milk crate. In the closet, dirty clothes were in sloppy piles on the floor. Nothing was hanging up on a few naked wire hangers. I rummaged through the musty clothes, then I looked on the closet shelf and found an old blue Adidas box.

I pulled it down, opened it, and found folded papers and old photos. Some of them had been taken in the projects, others had been taken in other locations, like downtown Chicago, New York City, Los Angeles, and Las Vegas. All the photos featured niggas and bitches in clothes from the 80s, they were rocking shit like MCM, Troop, Used and Damaged, and Todd 1. Occasionally, I spotted somebody in Gucci, Louis Vuitton, and Coach. I flipped through a few more photos. I saw one that had been taken in front of a hotel bed. On top of this hotel, bed was a pile of leather wallets, gold, diamond jewelry, credit cards, check books, and airplane ticket stubs to multiple cities. The photo I flipped to after that one was the one that caught my attention. I walked out of the bedroom, back into the living room, where Cat Eyes and Sneak were still busy beating the old crackhead nigga bloody.

"Sneak," I barked. "Check it out, Jo'?"

Sneak stopped mid-punch, took a deep breath, and came toward me. I held out the photo it was a picture of a gang of niggas in Adidas track suits, donkey ropes, and four-finger rings.

I asked Sneak, "You recognize any of these niggas?"

As soon as I got my question out, Sneak's eyes lit up.

He pointed to the dark-skinned nigga with the perm and said, "That's him, Gee. That's the nigga that shot Fatso." Sneak was excited

I knew he had to be right. "You sure, Jo'?" I asked with wrinkles on my forehead.

"Positive," Sneak said, nodding. "I don't forget faces."

I believed Sneak, but I still wanted his word confirmed. So, I walked across the floor and squatted down beside the old crackhead who was barely conscious and held the photo out in front of his face, pointing at the nigga with the perm.

"Is this Reggie Wade?"

"Yeah, that's him," the old crackhead said.

"Where is he?"

"I don't know. Understand me? He was here, but he left," the old nigga blurted.

"Where did he go?" I growled as I pulled out one of my .40s and put the cold barrel in his gut. "And before you open yo' fuckin' mouth to lie to me, I want you to feel this—"

Blocka!

I pulled the trigger and my .40 exploded in his gut, knocking all the wind out of him. He grunted, screamed, then doubled over clutching his wound.

I placed the hot, smoking, barrel to this temple. "I'm waiting for my answer?"

The old nigga squirmed, cringed, and winced. The bullet fragments inside him had him sweating like he was sitting in a sauna. He was struggling to keep his blood and guts from spilling out on the floor when he said, "I ain't sure where he is. Understand me? But before he left, he asked me where the ho' Streetlight was laying her head."

"And where is that?" I asked.

"The complex on—understand me? Thirty-sixth and Indiana."

I looked around at Cat Eyes, his green eyes sparkled like bicycle reflectors. Sneak's lip was curled when I looked at him. They felt like I felt. They felt like killing the muhfucka who had killed Fatso. Armed with the info I needed, I stood to my feet without a word, I turned and headed toward the door. My steps were quick, almost as if I was marching in a band. Before I could make it to the door, Cat Eyes stopped me. I spun around to see him and Sneak standing over the crumpled crackhead as he bled profusely.

Cat Eyes and Sneak had their Glocks out, their black hoodies had them looking like angels of death.

Cat Eyes pointed down at the old nigga with his Glock. "What you wanna do with this nigga, Folks?"

I thought for a hard second, and almost instantly I knew I needed to send a message. Not just to Reggie Wade but all the stick-up men in The Wells. The idea came to me like God revealed it to me.

"Toss his bitch ass out the window," I said coldly.

"Nooooo!" the old nigga yelled, as Cat Eyes and Sneak snatched him up by his legs and arms and held onto him like a battering ram.

I turned and walked out of the apartment, ran down the stairs and outta the building. Just as I made it to the Cutlass I heard a scream.

"Aaaaahhh!"

Then.

Splat!

A car alarm started crying like a hungry baby as I turned to see the old nigga, twisted, bloody, and laying on the caved-in hood of a powder blue, 85 Buick LeSabre. He was a bloody mess. He'd send a great message.

Streetlight. 36th and Indiana. I jumped into the Cutlass and prayed Reggie Wade was still there. I needed to end this shit now.

CHAPTER 15
REGGIE WADE

I popped out of the alley beside the little, white-brick, Arab store across the street from the yam orange-brick, low-rise complex on 36th and Indiana Avenue. A nice green lawn sprawled out around the place, huge trees with browning and yellowing leaves shot up. Around the buildings, and there were a couple of well-lit playgrounds, and parking lots full of cars in good condition. Wrought-iron bars and walking lamps were supposed to keep crime out, but that shit didn't work. Everything that went on in The Wells went on in the complex. The place didn't look so tough, but the niggas around the place did. Normally, I knew just how to deal with tough niggas. Tonight, however, I was trying to be low-key. I was here so the best thing to do was to be patient.

Patience was a virtue. I kicked a pile of empty bottles out of my way. Wine heads jumped on the alert. They were standing around a garbage-can fire with brown, paper bag-skirted wine bottles, shooting the shit. I walked past them, and they paid me no mind as I moved toward the entrance of the Arab store, which was nothing but a nook, a plexiglass window, and a revolving window for service this time of night. Fucked me up how the Arabs were scared to serve us at night, but they wasn't scared to take our scratch. It was a wonder, niggas still allowed them to do business here.

I bought a bottle of Bumpy Face, a pack of Newports, and a pack of mini-flavored Certs. Then I walked out of the store and joined the wine heads around the garbage can fire.

"See, what you cats don't realize is America's all about power and control. It always has been, and it always will be. The one

116

with the most power can exercise the most control," those words came out of a nigga in a dusty apple hat and overcoat with lips as pink as a monkey's ass.

He took a swig of his bottle. I could tell whatever he was drinking was strong as a muhfucka cause, after the swig, his monkey ass puckered like it was pinching off a turd. Afterward, he said, "Power and control is the concept that holds this house of cards together. Without that shit, all of this here country would be one big mess from the top down. Can you dig it, baby?" Pink lips said, looking at the wine head on his right.

That wine head was wearing a nappy beanie and a dusty pea coat. His skin was discolored and mangled like he'd been in a fire.

Burned face told Pink Lips, "I'm pickin' up what you puttin' down."

Pink Lips told him, "Be careful cause it's heavy, baby. Just think about it. The police here to keep us niggas in line. That's control, baby. And every time niggas get outta control. They exercise their power. When the police lose control, they call in the more powerful national guard to get control. When the National Guard loses control, they call in the military," he said, then took another swig and continued, "The bigger the gun, the more power. The more power, the more control. That's the American way, baby. Gotta keep the slaves on the plantation."

The other wine heads was out on their feet, but they nodded to second Pink Lips motion. Neither one of them minded me one bit. I just stood there half-listening to them as I drank Bumpy Face, smoked squares, and scanned the area around the complex for any sign of Streetlight.

Where this trick ass bitch at? It was well after 1:00 a.m. when I finally spotted her. She was power walking up The Ave, swinging a black, patent-leather handbag, blowing chewing gum bubbles. The bitch had gained a little weight since I'd last seen her, but it was her. A tight, tan maxi coat rode her thick curves like a caddy around the last turn on Lake Shore Drive. Knee-high, patent-leather riding boots matched her handbag and gave her that *come fuck me* stride. An Egyptian-style wig with a lot of inches was over heavy mascara, lashes, and black lipstick. Either the bitch was selling pussy or she was selling pussy. There wasn't no in-between.

The bitch moved quickly toward the complex like she'd had a bad night. Little did the bitch know, I was about to make her bad night worse. Anger settled on my ass like a bad-ass hangover. It made my insides hot, it made my head beat like a fucking bass drum. This bitch Streetlight had broken bad on me when I was at my lowest. I'd never forgive the bitch for that shit.

I waited for Streetlight to walk through the wrought-iron fence of the complex. Then I passed Pink Lips what was left of my Bumpy face. He tipped his hat and smiled with a set of chops that reminded me of a broken rake. After that, I thumped the butt of my square to the ground and with the hawk at my back, I marched through a break in oncoming traffic, crossed The Ave, and followed Streetlight into the complex.

I crept behind her, careful to stay enough feet in her rear as not to expose my hand too early. From where I was, I could see her fat ass struggling to free itself from her coat. The bitch still had that big ole ass. I crept closer. As she walked through the parking lot, up a paved walkway, and around the corner of one of the yam-orange low-rise buildings. I turned the corner behind her and smelled her scent in the wind. I saw an open glass door swinging shut. I darted to the glass door, stuck a boot between it, and the metal door frame. This was an old stick-up trick. Muhfuckas hardly ever looked back to see if a swinging door had shut behind them.

Inside the building, I tracked the bitch by her scent. That shit took me up a first-floor hallway and around a corner. I saw her before she saw me. She must've felt my presence at the end of the hallway cause she looked my way in the middle of keying herself into her crib.

I smiled at her with my whole face. "Hey, Nicolette," I called her by her government name. I did that cause I knew she hated it.

She didn't smile. "How you find out where I live, Reginald?"

"Damm, boo-boo," I said like I was offended. I held my arms out. "You don't sound happy to see me?"

She rolled her eyes and a sound escaped her that reminded me of a city bus. Her shoulders fell, too. The bitch was not happy to see me. She asked, "What you doin' here, Reginald?" She turned around, put her back on her apartment door, and crossed her arms. "What do you want?"

I took slow steps toward her kinda like a leopard creeping up on a water hole full of impalas. "Come on, Boo-Boo. Don't act like that. We loved each other once upon a time. I still got a thang for yo' punk ass. We ain't seen each other in five years." I closed the space between us. "You mean to tell me, you don't miss me? Not even a little bit?"

She smiled. I had her.

I told her, "Go ahead and open the door. I got some dope. I know you got Golden Champagne in the fridge. It's been five years, Boo-Boo. Let's sit down and catch up on all that lost time?"

I tried to read the bitch, but reading her had always been hard. I had taught her ass too much when we was together. Now that I wasn't with the bitch, it was working against me.

A nigga gotta watch it with how much he schools a bitch.

Streetlight's face stayed expressionless for a moment. Then she turned around and opened the door. I followed her inside and locked up behind us. When my back was turned my lips curled in anger. I swallowed that shit back down. It tasted like poison on my stomach. When I turned around I had my costume on again.

The bitch unzipped her boots, kicked 'em off, and I followed her as she led me deeper into her crib, hitting light switches along the way. No matter what the punk bitch did in the streets, I could see she still kept a clean house. She had furnished her new crib with some Rent-A-Center shit she'd probably had delivered to the old crib before she moved out. Either way, it was a bunch of cheap shit, but it was well put together on a nut-colored carpet that didn't budge under my boots.

"Go ahead and have a seat in the living room," she told me. "I'll be out in a sec," she said, then disappeared into the kitchen.

I took a seat on the paisley sofa. I heard tap water running. I heard glasses clinking. I heard the fridge open with a suctioned kiss and close with another one. After that, the punk bitch came walking into the living room with two glasses in her hands and a chilled bottle of Golden Champagne cradled in her arm. Her Egyptian-style wig was gone. In its place as a blond Caesar, waves spinning, perfect lining. I had to say, the haircut fitted the bitch. She'd look perfect with it in her casket. She sat the glass down on the cocktail table, poured us up, then flopped down on the other end of the sofa with one leg tucked under her fat ass. Cheap perfume went to my brain.

I told her, "Girl, bring yo' ass over here. Ain't nobody gon' bite you."

She told me, "Nall, I'm good right here," with a lot of attitude.

I let her be, I pulled out my pack of squares, my lighter, and what was left of the bundle of dope I had on me.

Then I sat that shit on the cocktail table.

Streetlight looked at the bundle of dope. Then she looked back up at me and said, "I see you already back out here on yo' bullshit."

I tried to throw the bitch off, "What bullshit you talkin' bout, Boo-Boo?"

She threw a hand at me. "Don't even try it, sweetie. You know we don' been there and done that. I can write a book about you."

"You need to get to writin', then," I told her. "Cause any book with Reggie Wade in it gon' be a New York Times Bestseller," I said, then laid some blows out on the cocktail table.

The bitch asked me, "When you get out?"

I told her, "I been out for a while now. You woulda known that if you wouldn't have broken bad on me."

"Broke bad on you?" She turned up her nose and repeated, "Ain't nobody break bad on you, sweetie. You broke bad on yo' self. I was willin' to be there for yo' stubborn ass as a friend, but you wanted me to live out here like I was locked up in there with you. I told you I wasn't that bitch. Please understand, sweetie? You broke bad on me. I didn't break bad on you."

I wasn't tryna buy that slum she was selling. She could turn somebody else's neck green with that weak ass shit. She knew what it meant to fuck with a real nigga like me. She had jumped in the car to enjoy the perks, then she'd hopped out when it was time to put in the work. A nigga gotta keep his eye on a thirsty ass bitch. She'll run off on you when you need her the most. Streetlight was a thirsty ass bitch and I was collecting on that debt she owed me tonight.

I tore off a piece of my Newport box. I used that to scoop some dope for Streetlight. She took a one-on-one and I finished the scoop off. After that, I fired up a square.

"But all that shit is in the past," I told her, smiling and lying through my teeth. I clutched my nuts and squeezed the heat there. "We're here together now and ain't nothin' like the now. Let's take advantage of the moment. It's called the present cause it's a gift."

"Sweetie, don't be comin' at me with that bull shit you read in prison," she said.

"I ain't tryna run no game on you, Nicolette—"

"Stop callin' me that!"

"I'm just tryna get some of that gushy shit I been missin'," I told her, grabbing my dick.

I could feel my shit pushin' up against the inside of my pants. I was salty at the bitch, but I still wanted to fuck her big, thick ass.

"I ain't even got my nut out the sand, yet."

She threw another hand at me, rolled her eyes, smacked her lips, and said, "You can run that shit to a marathon, Sweetie. I

121

know you don' found some pussy to stick that greedy dick of yours in."

I smiled, "So my dick greedy, huh?"

She didn't answer, she just looked at me for a long moment. I saw her mind working.

Suddenly, she leaped up off the sofa. "Uh-uh," she said, shaking her head. "We ain't doin' this, Sweetie."

"Doin' what?" I said like I was confused. I knew damn well what the bitch was saying, but I'd come too fucking far to let this shit slip through my hands now.

"It was nice seein' you again, Reginald," she told me as she backed away from the sofa. "But you gotta go."

That shit hit me outta nowhere like a sniper's bullet.

I stayed seated.

She folded her arms and tapped her foot to a nervous beat.

"Boo-Boo," I said as soft as a fly's landing. "I ain't got nowhere to go. You know Momma Cynt passed when I was down."

"What about your Sista, Rachel?"

"What about her? She ain't got her shit together."

"So, where you been stayin'?"

"I been crashin' over at the men's shelter down on State Street," I told her. "It's almost three in the mornin', Boo-Boo." She needed to be worked on a little more. I kept the pressure on her to stop the bleeding like a gunshot wound. "I tell you what, Boo-Boo...lemme crash right here on the couch. I'll stay out here, I swear. And as soon as the sun comes up I'll leave. I'll get outta your way." I licked a finger and made a cross on my chest. "So, help me, God."

A stiff moment passed. Then, "You don't even believe in God, Sweetie, but whatever," she said. "Anyways, you can go 'head and sleep on the couch. I ain't gon' put you out in the middle of the night. That would be some cruel shit. But first thing in the mornin' yo' ass is outta here, Sweetie. We is not doin' this."

122

I agreed to Streetlight terms. Then she left me alone on the sofa. After that, I snorted more dope, smoked more squares, and drank the rest of the Golden Champagne.

In her bedroom, I could hear Keith Sweat singing *There's a Right And Wrong Way To Love Somebody*. The shower came on and ran for about twenty minutes, then cut off. Soon after that, I heard feet padding through the hallway. She had taken a quick shower. I thought about her black ass, thick as Karo Syrup, naked as muhfucka. The thought had me massaging my hard dick through my pants.

After fifteen anxious minutes of this, I leaped off the sofa, tip-toed out of the living room, through the hallway, and down to Streetlight's bedroom door. It was cracked, I peeped inside and saw her on her bed. Some yellow glow from the light that hung from the corner of the building across from her, shined through her bedroom window and made her sweaty skin resemble glazed chocolate. Her eyes were closed, both her lips were inside her mouth, her nipples were hard, and her legs were spread wide as the sky. She moaned and groaned under the music as she used the three, middle fingers of her right hand to rub slow circles on her clit. At the same time, she used her left hand to stroke her wet pussy with a purple, 12-inch dildo. I unbuckled, unzipped, and whipped my hard dick out right there. I stroked my dick and watch the bitch please herself. She came. Then she beat her fist on the bed in frustration and crawled out of bed. Quickly, I turned, tiptoed back through the hallway, back into the living room, and laid down on the sofa. I closed my eyes just she as came walking in on me.

"Don't be tryna play possum," she said. "I saw you at my door."

I opened my eyes. Her chocolate skin was oiled like tanned leather. Her large, hard nipples looked like black diamonds. She had a little pudge around her gut, some stretch marks, too. But that shit wasn't fucking nothing up. I looked down between her legs and her fleshy pussy lips were puckering out from behind a thin rug of curls. The bitch still had the body that made her street famous, I was about to enjoy this shit.

She told me, "I hope you didn't buss a nut on my carpet. Get that dope and bring yo' as in this room."

She said and turned on her heels. "Boo-Boo gon' tighten you up."

Out of my clothes, I stood on the side of the bed in front of Streetlight. The bitch had my hard dick in her hand, stroking it. "Got damn, Sweetie!" she blurted. "I almost forgot how big your dick was."

I'd given her a bag of dope. She poured it out in a line that ran from the base to the top of my hard dick. Then she snorted the line and licked off the residue. She spit on me and slurped me in her warm wet mouth. The warmness of her mouth, the wetness of her saliva, the slurping sounds she made as she stroked me and sucked me, to my highest heights. I grabbed the back of her head and showed her where to find my nut.

She found that spot and stayed there, squeezing, twisting, and sucking until I came in her mouth, bucking and grunting.

She let me go and laughed.

I asked, "What you laughing at?"

She told me. "You ain't changed a bit. You still can't last a minute in this mouth."

"You got that," I told her, pushing her back onto the bed. "That first one was on me. But the second, third, and fourth one is on you."

She looked me up and down like I needed vouchers. "Whatever, Sweetie, we'll see."

I climb on top of her. She opened her legs and swung them up. I cuffed the back of her thighs in the crooks between my biceps and forearms. Then I slid into her wet pussy and started stroking.

I told her, "When I was in the joint, I used to dream about this pussy and beat my dick."

"Well, you ain't gotta beat your dick no more," she told me. "Beat this pussy."

"You sure you want me to do that?" I asked as I thrust inside her.

She moaned, "Umm-hmm...hell...fuckin'...yeah!"

I pulled my dick out of her and stroked myself as I told her to get on all fours, she rubbed circles on her clit as she obeyed me. The smell of her pussy was strong in the air. Keith Sweat's crying ass was singing *How Deep is Your Love*. When Streetlight was in front of me on all fours. I entered her pussy from behind, slapped her fat ass cheeks till they danced, and fucked her till she trembled and came. She was still in the chokehold of her release when I grabbed her wrists, held her arms out like bicycle handlebars, and with no warning, the grimiest grit curled my lips into a scowl, my wet dick plopped out of her creaming pussy and stabbed her in her tight asshole. I was up in her back door to my balls by the time she screamed.

"Aaaahhhh! Shit! No!" her shrieking could've woken the dead and made a deaf muhfucka hear.

"Bitch!" I growled with each rough stab in her asshole. "I...was...nothin'...but—" I gave her my hard dick to the balls.

"Aaaahhh!" she yelled.

"—a good...nigga—" I pulled out of her to the tip. "—to...you—" I stabbed her ass hard.

"Aaahhh!" she yelled. "Please...Reginald...please...no!"

She looked back at me with tears in her eyes. I spit in the bitch's face. I needed the bitch to know how she made me feel when she left me at my lowest. That shit hurt like a big dick in the ass.

I held onto her wrists tight as I rode her asshole rough as a BMX down the side of a rocky mountain. She screamed at the top of her lungs, it was a scream that came from the depths of her soul. The louder she screamed, the more excited I became and the more excited I became, the harder I pounded her asshole. She tried to snatch away from me and crawl outta my grasp. I caught the bitch and beat her ribs like a bass drum. She collapsed, I kept riding her asshole so fucking hard that her ass cheeks hitting my stomach sounded like firecrackers.

I fucked her like that till my nut tingled at the top of my dick. "You hurt the shit outta me, Nicolette," I told her, mad at myself for letting her know how bad she'd made me feel when she left me. "I loved yo' dirty drawers, but now it's fuck you bitch. Take every inch of this dick in your ass."

I stabbed her in the ass repeatedly. She grunted from the gut at the end of every stroke. Then finally, I came in the bitch's ass and started choking her from behind.

After I let her go she coughed and fainted. I pulled my dick out of her ass, along with her hemorrhoids, blood, shit, and cum. I wiped my dick off with her sheets, then crawled out of bed and jumped back into my gear.

I was standing beside her bed with The Beast pointed at her face when she came to. "All that shit I told you while I was fuckin' you earlier was a lie, bitch," I growled. "I thought about you true enough. But when I thought about you it wasn't nothin' sexual about my thought—"

"Reggie," she cried. "Why you doin' me like this?"

"When I thought about you," I told her as I leveled the barrel of The Beast with the bitch's grill. "All I thought about was blowin' yo' muhfuckin' brains out."

"Reggie, Sweetie...please...don't do this," she cried.

I ignored her cries and her pleas. "You knew I played for keeps," I told her. "Scars for scabs, bitch!"

Boom!

The Beast let out an orange and blue blast, the bitch's head exploded like a pinata full of brains and blood. The bloodstains on the wall and the bed looked like the results of red paintballs. My job was done here. The barrel of The Beast smoked as I felt it fall to my thigh. Then I turned around and walked outta Streetlight's bedroom.

The chapter of revenge was over in the book of my life. Now, I was free to look forward without constantly looking back. You know what they say about that, constantly looking back makes a nigga miss the shit that's right in front of him.

CHAPTER 16
DONTAE

CPD patrol cars and unmarked police vehicles were everywhere when I finally pulled up on The Ave. Bluecoats was busy keeping a crowd of spectators in check as I parked and hopped out of the Cutlass. I scanned the scene and instantly knew what happened. Reggie Wade had struck again.

This time he'd killed the trick bitch Streetlight. The bitch with the best head in the city had caught a bad one.

Parked along The Ave was a blue Astrovan. I knew the driver, so I crossed the street and found Big Jubilee Jackson there beside his ride, smoking a huge spliff. I approached him and gave him the GD handshake.

Jubilee was in authority over the GDs on The Ave which was a separate set from The Wells, but we still were familiar with one another. His huge hand swallowed mine like a lion's mouth.

"What up, Big Jube?"

"Ain't shit, Tae Murder."

Jubilee was a big nigga. He was built like an offensive lineman and tipped the scale at about 350lbs. He was tall with that shit, too. The big Triple Fat Goose parka with the fox fur around the hood made him look like The Yeti.

I looked around at the crowd. The people were rubbernecking to try to see something...anything. It was crazy how muhfuckas was obsessed with violence. Nosy muhfuckas stayed in everything but a casket.

I turned back to Big Jubilee. "Fuck happened out here, Jo' ?"

Jubilee hit his spliff and said, "I think a muhfucka offed the bitch Streetlight. A nigga told me he heard a loud blast he thought was a shotgun."

Jubilee's words affirmed my previous assumptions, Reggie Wade had got up with Streetlight and bussed her shit.

I knew he holding on to some type of animosity toward me. Streetlight had been right. But I knew she hadn't estimated that Reggie Wade would kill her for leaving him while he was in the joint. The shit just seemed all too petty. She probably had known him better than anyone alive. She should've been able to see the play before he brought it to her door.

I shook my head and thought about asking Jubilee if he or anybody else had seen the shooter, but I knew I couldn't ask him that. Niggas just didn't ask those kinds of questions in the streets, not unless you wanted to be viewed as a snitch.

I shook up with Jubilee and walked away from the scene. My chances of catchin' up with Reggie Wade tonight had ended. A sick feeling crept in my gut that made me feel like I'd eaten something spoiled, and I had. The spoiled shit I'd ate was called shit. My nose flared, my top lip curled, my heartbeat raced. Reggie Wade got away from me twice in one night. Anger was bitter on my tongue.

I had to take that shit out on somebody.

****

"Oh-my-fuckin'-God, mister," Princess moaned and groaned as she rubbed slow circles around her clit and threw that ass back at me fast and hard.

"You-are-fuckin'-the-shit-outta...ooohhh...me!"

I was behind Princess, holding tight as vice grips to her soft waist, eyes closed, face to the ceiling, lips pulled into my mouth, sweating and stroking. I was in her deep and fast, hard thrusts that knocked sparks off her ass. A line of drool, fell from the corner of my open mouth, onto her sweaty back. I bent down over her, never missing a stroke, and licked that shit off her spine. She shivered, trembled, and came with a high-pitched scream. After she came, I turned her onto her back, threw her legs on my shoulders, and slid inside her again.

She took the dick like a porn star, stuck her pussy-wet fingers in my mouth. I sucked them and licked her 'till I busted my nut. My stroke stuttered and stammered as I emptied my nuts inside her slippery pussy. Finally, weakened by the release of my pinned-up anger, I rolled off Princess and laid beside her as we both took a moment to catch our breath.

"That was some savage ass shit, mister," Princess gasped. "What's up with you?"

She rolled over and looked at me.

Wet hair was stuck by sweat to the side of her face. Her hazel eyes were twinkling like night stars. She braced her head on her hand waiting for me to talk.

I told her, "This shit with Reggie Wade got me pissed off."

"I knew somethin' was botherin' you."

I frowned. "It's just—I been tryna catch the nigga and buss his shit," I told her. "But the nigga keeps gettin' away."

"Don't rush it, bae," Princess told me. "Just be patient. Believe it or not, that nigga ain't gettin' away. When it's his time to pay for what he did, he won't be able to get away."

I nodded. "You right."

She leaned in and gave me a wet kiss with a lotta tongue.

Then she pulled her lips back and told me, "In the meantime in-between time, I'ma help you get your mind off that shit."

"If that's possible."

She slithered down my body, grabbed my dick, licked it, and looked up at me. "Oh, it's possible, bae," she said. "Shooo...if this head can't clear your mind, nothin' can."

She stuck the dick in her mouth and went to work. But the whole time I was thinkin' about murder. I thought about the photo in my jacket. I knew what I had to do to turn up the heat.

Princess spit the dick out and looked up at me. "Your mind clear, yet?"

I told her, "Almost, bae."

CHAPTER 17
ANGIE

I almost kissed Dontae. That shit had come out of nowhere, too. It was a temporary moment of weakness. At least I think it was. I know if I had kissed my dead baby daddy's best friend, my best friend's man. I would've been wrong on so many levels. I really don't know what came over me. Maybe it's the way Dontae walks, the way he talks, the way he dresses, his mannerisms—everything about him reminds me of Fatso. Being around him makes me realize Fatso not only admired him, but his admiring Dontae had made him commit the highest form of flattery, Imitation.

Fatso was a carbon copy while Dontae was the real thing.

This had to be the cause of me being attracted to him.

Then, he'd been helpful beyond his responsibility. He paid for Fatso's funeral, gave his mother money, and he'd been takin' care of me and my son. Dontae is an example of extreme loyalty and principle. This and more, I believe, is the reason I almost kissed him.

Y'all judging me now cause y'all don't understand. That nigga is fine, for real, for real. He got that smooth, peanut-butter skin, and he got good hair. That he always wears in two thick braids down the side of his head. His eyes are a deep brown. You can look in them and see passion and strength, and those lips...oh, my God! For real, for real...those lips...uh-uh-uh. I just wanna rub my pussy all over those big muhfuckas 'til I cum. This how I'm feeling when he sits with me, gets close to me, rubs my back, grabs my face, and uses his thumbs to wipe the tears from my eyes. He was right there holding me, touching me, and comforting me right at the very moment when I needed to be comforted the most. That shit made my pussy wet and I ain't gon' fake the funk, I felt an itch that I seriously needed him to scratch.

I know he saw the need in my eyes cause I saw it in his, too. For a split second, the feeling between us was mutual. However, in that split second, we'd both allowed our better judgment to kick in and did the right thing. If denying ourselves that moment was the right thing.

It was early Halloween morning when I woke up to the sun in my eyes. I had promised Rashaun I'd take him to buy a costume and Halloween candy, so I crawled out of bed in white, lace panties, and nothing else, and went to Rashaun's bedroom door to check on him. He was in bed, asleep on his belly just like his dad.

Good.

Momma needed some time to herself before the long day of costumes, candy, and trick-or-treating.

I closed Rashaun's bedroom door, making sure it kissed the door frame quietly, as not to awaken him. Then I turned and walked into the pink bathroom and locked the door behind me. Once I was alone in the bathroom, I turned on the hot water in the tub and ran the hottest bath I could run. Steam filled up the bathroom, fogged the mirror over the sink, and warmed my body. I poured an apple bubble bath from Bath and Body Works into the tub, and when the white pillow of foam came spilling over the lip of the tub, I turned the water off and stuck a toe into the bathwater to test its heat. The water burned my toe. It was hot enough for me. Satisfied that the water was to my specificity, I rolled my panties down over my hips, down over my thighs, down over my legs. When they were at my ankles, I stepped out of 'em and climbed into the bathtub. Once my body was submerged in hot water, I grabbed my razor from the side of the tub. Next, I shaved my arms pit, my legs, and my pussy, till all those womanly parts of me were nice and smooth. Then I returned my razor, picked up my Dove bar and washcloth, and lathered it up. I lathered my body till every part of me was covered with moisturizing soap. The moment I began washing my pussy I began thinking about Dontae.

Before I knew it, I was using my fingers on myself. I rubbed my clit in slow circles with one hand and penetrated my wet pussy with the two fingers of my other hand. That shit felt so good, I closed my eyes and visualized Dontae's big lips nibbling on my clit, sucking on the inner and outer lips of my pussy, and sticking his tongue inside my tight pussy hole. I bit down on my bottom lip and moaned as I fantasized about the length and width of his dick. I wondered how it would feel inside of me?

"Uummm...hmmm...uuummm...oooh shit!" I moaned as I felt my pussy about to squirt its juices. "Ooooohhh, Dontae!" I found myself callin' his name as my orgasm sent me into shivering spasms and curled my toes.

I rubbed my clit till it became too sensitive for me to touch. Then I left it alone and let it tingle and throb as I used two fingers to penetrate and squeeze my pussy lips. I came enough to fill up the tub. The release felt sweet. It relaxed me, and that moment of tantalizing ecstasy, I forgot about Fatso and his tragic death. All I thought about now was me and what I needed for me to feel whole again. I needed Dontae.

CHAPTER 18
DETECTIVE STEVEN KNOX

"The victim is back here in the bedroom, Steve," Jill said as she gestured for me to follow her.

She looked good today. Her hair was parted up the middle of her head and cascaded down around her breast and back. A chic, black leather Maxi and a tight pair of blue jean leggings accentuated her every womanly curve. Black leather boots with a low heel, and the gap between her thighs made her bottom half look like she enjoyed riding horses. I had to get some of that pussy.

I was thinking about fucking Jill from the back as she led me through the hallway at an apartment in the orange-brick, low-rise complex on 36th and Indiana. I'd been en route to the Ida B. Wells Housing Projects when I'd gotten the call to respond to another homicide in the area.

So, here I was, following big booty ass Jill into another room that smacked me dead in the face with the stench of death. The body of a dark-skinned woman was sprawled out across the bed. Her head had been almost completely blown off her neck. Blood had coagulated everywhere. The scene of this murder reminded me of two other murder scenes I had currently started investigating.

Jill said, "It looks like a rape slash murder. The victim is thirty-two-year-old Nicolette Robinson."

I nodded slowly. "Hmm...Streetlight."

"You know her?"

"She's a prostitute. The ex-girlfriend of an old acquaintance of mine," I told Jill as I pulled a pen out and used it to pick up a little Ziploc bag.

I'd found another bag with little bomb logos on it at another murder scene. This made the third time, so I knew the chances this recurrence was some kind of coincidence was out of the window.

The other day I'd found out Reggie Wade had been released from the Maximum State Prison at Statesville. Since he'd been out, I'd responded to three different murder scenes where all the victims had been blasted to pieces by shotgun slugs, which just so happened to be Reggie Wade's weapon of choice. Couple that with the fact that I kept finding little Ziploc bags with bomb logos on 'em, and I was dealing with a string of drug-related homicides that, if I let get out of control, would become a fucking war in the streets.

"What you got?" Jill asked me.

I told her, "I don't know, yet but it looks like it got somethin' to do with a heroin bag over in the Ida B. Wells. That and an old stick-up man that was just released from prison a couple of months ago." I said, then dropped the little Ziploc bag off the end of my pen and walked over to her.

I looked at Jill, her eyebrows met in the middle of her head. She was a practical woman. She needed clear answers to everything, but this world hardly ever offered clear answers. This fact upset women like Jill. She didn't know how to deal with unanswered questions for even a moment.

She told me, "I'll take care of things here, and have a full report on your desk by morning."

I told her, "Thanks." Then I walked toward the door, but before I walked out, I turned around and said, "Jill?"

She looked up at me with curious brown eyes. "Yes?"

"Aye," I said tryna pick my words wisely. "Why don't you prepare your report and we can go through it over dinner? You pick the place."

She looked me up and down with knowing eyes, then smirked and said, "Dinner, huh?"

I held up my hands in submission. "Just dinner," I told her with a flirtatious smile.

She thought it over a moment.

Her thinking process was so long I thought she'd turn me down.

Finally, she nodded and told me, "Okay, we can do dinner."

Then, I can do you.

"Your pick. My treat. Just call me with the details."

"I'ma take you up on that," she said with a smirk. "I sure will."

I walked out of the bedroom on a natural high. That natural high didn't last long at all. I needed to hit the streets. I wanted to get out in front of these murders before they got out in front of me. I knew exactly where to start.

CHAPTER 19
CAT EYES

"Forty-Eights!"

The brown box Chevy that hit the corner on 37th Street needed no introduction. Everybody on the block knew Faggot Steve was coming.

Damn!

I didn't feel like dealing with his shit. Not on a blustery and rainy Halloween afternoon.

The puss' ass, dick in the booty muhfucka gunned the engine of the car and hopped the curb. When the car came to a screeching stop, Faggot Steve hopped out. He had on a wrinkled, brown leather jacket, faded stonewash jeans, and New Balance 510s the color of old blood.

"Get outta that hole!" Lil Tonio screamed as the dick ran up on the building letting the pitcher know the dicks was downstairs. Faggot Steve ran right past me, gritting on Lil' Tonio.

"Bring yo' lil ass here," he told Lil' Tonio as he fingered him over to him.

Lil Tonio gritted back on his ass. "Fuck you! You swine ass faggot! I ain't comin' nowhere!" Lil Tonio shouted.

Faggot Steve rushed Lil Tonio and slapped fire from him. The blow knocked shorty's skully off his head, and damn near snapped his neck. Lil Tonio grabbed his cheek, tears welled in his eyes. He was huffing and puffing like he'd just ran the 40-yard dash.

"Come on, Steve. You ain't have to hit him like that!" I snapped. "He ain't nothin' but thirteen!"

"So muhfuckin' what!" Faggot Steve growled, still mugging Lil Tonio. "You teach yo' lil' worker to stay in a child's place. Now, gon' get yo' lil' ass the fuck away from this building. You lil crack baby."

Lil Tonio didn't budge, he just stood there looking at Faggot Steve like he could kill his ass. If he'd had a gun on him, he would've probably tried.

A few customers rolled up and saw the dick car parked sideways and knew what it was hitting for. A few more walk-throughs hit the corner and saw our stand-off with Faggot Steve and got somewhere. This shit was bad for business. I was willing to do anything to get Faggot Steve's puss' ass away from the spot.

I told Lil Tonio, "Gon' be up, shorty."

Faggot Steve jacked his jeans. His gun holster bounced a little. If he was tryna spook Lil Tonio that shit didn't work and he looked pissed about it.

Lil Tonio mugged Faggot Steve and walked away. "You got that swine," he said. "I'll see you again."

"That'll be the day yo' ass don't see fourteen, bitch!" Faggot Steve growled. "Try me?"

The second Lil Tonio was gone, Faggot Steve turned his attention to me. "On the wall!" he ordered. "Spread 'em, nigga, you know the drill!"

"You know I ain't dirty, Steve," I told him. "What's up?"

He shoved me in my chest. I flew, back into the wall. "I said on the wall!" he barked.

His bitch ass was on his period today. Furious, I turned around, placed my palms on the wall and spread my legs. Faggot Steve frisked me, then stood beside me and fired up a cancer stick.

After that, he looked at me with this shitty ass grin and asked, "Where Dontae at?"

I told him, "It ain't my day to babysit him."

"Oh," he grunted like he was irritated. "You wanna be smart, huh? You wanna be smart, muhfucka? I'll stay out here all day, and y'all won't sell another bag out this muhfucka!"

I blew out my frustration. "I don't know where that nigga at, Steve?"

He blew smoke in my grill. That shit almost set me off. "Would you tell me where he was at if you knew?" he asked with a smirk.

I didn't answer, I just looked at his faggot ass like he was a hunnid different kind of slow.

He said, "That's what I thought."

He smoked as I stood there anxious to be let go. He was talking to me too long, and the last thing I wanted was for muhfuckas to get the wrong idea. When Faggot Steve talked to you and people saw it, they automatically assumed you were snitching, or you were gay. I was neither, so I was anxious as a muhfucka for him to let me go.

"I'm clean, Steve," I said. "Can I go?"

"Depends."

"On what?" I said, frowning cause I knew he was on some bullshit.

"What you know about that nigga that did the Nestea Plunge out the sixth-floor window, over at the seven-twenty-seven building?"

Faggot Steve asked me that shit, and I took a second to look in his eyes. He didn't know shit. He was here on a fishing expedition.

I told him, "I don't fuck around at the seven-twenty-seven building. If you wanna know about that building then why the fuck you way over here?"

He puffed his cancer stick down to the filter. Then gritted on me as he thumped the filter to the ground. His little boo-game was soft ass a muhfucka.

Faggot Steve just told me, "Get the fuck outta here, Cat Eyes. This shit closed down for the day."

I was made to walk away, but as soon as my foot hit the front steps of the building.

Faggot Steve told me, "When you see Dontae tell him I need to ask him why I keep findin' his Bomb in a Bag dope bags on my murder scenes."

I kept walking but I took note of everything Faggot Steve said. His bitch ass was a sneaky muhfucka. Dontae needed to know what was going on with his ass ASAP.

CHAPTER 20
PRINCESS

It had been over three weeks since my girl Angie had been out of the house, so I went by and scooped her up, then we scooped up Keisha, Cat Eyes baby momma and headed for the boutiques along Michigan Avenue Magnificent Mile. Angie had been a little sad at first. I could tell Fatso's death was still weighing heavy on her mind. The day wasn't helping her mood either. It was windy and rainy, but then again it was late October and it was always windy and rainy during that time in the city. So, yeah, me and Keisha set about to cheer Angie up. We ran through Neiman Marcus, Nordstroms, and Saks Fifth Avenue. We tried on all the Gucci, Louis V, and Prada in the ladies' department. This bitch Keisha's thirsty ass even started boosting and shit, which I knew she'd do. That was why I scooped her ass in the first place. Even though I didn't really fuck with the bitch like that, I enjoyed the perks of her five-finger discount. You ain't gotta really fuck with somebody like that to take gifts from 'em. Do you?

Anyways, we shopped till we muhfuckin' dropped, then we ended up in House of Style & Beauty hair and nail salon, a trendy little shop tucked into a storefront between J & J's Fish and Jammin' Two's, on 35th Street. The strip was busy as hell outside the huge picture window of the shop. A dude in a black tux was sitting on a crate playing a Casio keyboard. Street vendors were out selling everything from socks to watches. The usual drug traffic moved under the cover of all the legal hustle going on. Inside the shop were nothing but a row of chairs and mirrors, a countertop and cabinets which held all of the stylist tools and hair care products, a couple of red-leather sofas that appeared to be from the 70s, and a small table covered with back issues of Ebony, Jet, and Essence magazines.

Kim, a half black-half-Korean chick from the Southwest side appeared at the glass door of the shop, and Liv, the girl doing my hair hit a buzzer and let her in. Liv was an amazon bitch with a red mohawk, tats, and piercings everywhere. The bitch even had one on the hood of her clit. Do not ask me how I found that shit out.

She was a wired bitch. Not my kinda people, but sista girl could lay some hair. So, it is what it is.

Kim walked in with wine and spirits. She was the one that had the place smelling like nail polish remover over Hawaiian Silk perm. After she popped open a bottle of Hen and poured everyone a glass, we drank till our tongues got loose as a goose.

"Angie," Yonna said as she placed burgundy highlights in Angie's hair. "How you been, girl? I heard about your son's father. These niggas nowadays don't know how to do nothin' but be jealous."

"That shit hurt me down to my core, girl," Angie said. "But I'm really hurt for my son. He'll never know what it's like to grow up with his father."

Yonna took a break to sip from her glass. She's a big girl, one of those chicks that'd squeeze into some shit she knew she ain't have no business wearing. I gave her ass evil eyes to get her to change the subject. I had bought Angie to the shop to get her mind off Fatso, not to have her talking about a dead man all day.

Jazzmeen the redbone chick doing Kiesha's hair picked up on the vibe.

Jazzmeen and Kiesha's mothers were sisters, so they favored each other a lot. Both of them hos had that creole shit going on with them. You know? That gray-eyed and good hair shit. All Kiesha ever had to do with her hair was get it pressed. Her hair belonged on a badder bitch like me.

"But one thing you have to do is learn how to live again without that person," Jazzmeen chimed in. "It can be hard, but it's a few ways to do it."

"Yeah," Kiesha interrupted. "Like findin' new dick."

"Bitch, shut up," Angie blurted. "Dick is the answer for all your problems."

"No," Liv said. "I think Keisha's actually on to somethin' this time. I read in a magazine, that grief can be overcome with enjoyable sex."

"Angie, girl," Kim put her two cents in. "You don't wanna be like the women in Korea. My mother told me when a Korean woman's husband dies, she kills herself to go to the afterlife with him."

"What the fuck!" I snapped. "Why would a woman do some shit like that?"

Kim shrugged. "Don't get me to lyin'. But I think they just feel like they aren't good."

"See, bitch!" Kiesha blurted. "You don't wanna end up like a Korean bitch. Find you a dick, ride that muhfucka and suck that muhfucka 'till you get over your grief. The worst thing that can happen is that you'll be one satisfied bitch."

I looked at Angie, and it appeared she was thinking the advice over. I was thinking too about how I'd felt when my father died. I remember Dontae fucking me right outta that grief. I mean, I still missed my father, but I wasn't all broken up about that shit after Dontae put enough of that dick on me.

I told Angie, "Once you let another dude hit it. You won't feel so attached to Fatso anymore, bitch. If you love him, you know that they say, you gotta let him go."

Angie sipped from her glass, then said, "I can't do that shit. I can't just go out and get some random dude and just fuck him, just to be fuckin' him. That ain't me."

Keisha said, "Who said go get some random dude, bitch? You mean to tell me you ain't got you one nigga who always wanted to fuck, but you didn't let him 'cause you was with Fatso?"

I saw Angie thinking about that question. She had a nigga around like that. All bitches did. We were well into a great conversation about sex and grief when Liv turned my chair toward the picture window. That was when I saw her. She was looking into the window as if she had spotted me from outside and was trying to make sure it was me she'd spotted. Her trifling ass was a mess, too. She was wearing one of these green coats from the Army Surplus stores, and it was ripped at the right shoulder. The micro braids in her hair looked like stitches and her lips were dark and crusty as burned toast. When I acted like I didn't see her ass, she started smiling and waving.

Oh! I wished she would just go somewhere and die.

Angie said, "Ooh, girl, ain't that your cousin Mi-Mi?"

I said, "Yeah, that's her nothin' ass. She don't wanna do nothin' but beg. I ain't got time for her dirty ass. Stupid self, don' let some nigga turn her out on that crack."

Mi-Mi put her forehead on the window, cupped her hands, and looked in. "I know you see me, Princess!" she hollered through the window. "Don't be playing me to the left and shit!"

Liv said, "I'ma buzz her ass in, girl,"

I told her, "No, Liv, don't do that shit."

"Fuck that," Liv told me. "I don't need her makin' a scene out there. Just talk to her."

Buzz!

Liv hit the buzzer, Mi-Mi ran her happy ass to the door and came barging into the shop.

"What up, cuz?" Mi-Mi said with a wide smile and a goofy-ass wave.

I instantly got sick.

"Hey, Angie, Kiesha. Hey y'all," she spoke to everybody, then walked over to me. "You know you saw me tryna get your attention, cuz," Mi-Mi said. "What you think you too good for me now?"

I looked her ass up and down. She had on dusty jeans, old Tretons, and she'd lost a lotta weight since the last time I'd seen her. My cousin Comisha had been a pretty girl once upon a time. We had been close, too. But the last couple of years had made me kick her sorry ass to the curb. The bitch had gone from smoking weed to smoking crack on weed. This was a no-no, I couldn't fuck with no crack head bitches. Crack head bitches stole shit outta your purse and shit.

I rolled my eyes at her ass real stank-like. "What you want, Mi-Mi?"

She smiled and rocked her weight on one foot. "Damn, cuz," she blurted. "It's like that?"

I smacked my lips. "Yeah, it's like that. You know I can't fuck with you no more."

"Why?" she said as her smiled melted and dripped onto the floor. "What I do to you?"

"It ain't about what you did to me," I told her. "It's about what you did to you. I mean, look at you...you smokin' that shit. Your hair ain't been done, your nail polished all chipped and shit. I bet you in the streets suckin' niggas dicks for that shit now, huh?"

I could tell that my words were punching the bitch in the gut because her facial expression went through a million different changes.

"Princess, you ain't right," she said as if she was hurt.

I didn't give two fucks. She was embarrassing the shit outta me in front of people, so I was giving her dusty ass everything she had coming.

"And when's the last time you bathed?" I asked turning up my nose. "Your coochie probably stinkin' and shit. That rock got you lettin' yourself go like that? You need to get your shit together. I remember when I looked up to you. You was one of the baddest bitches around here. Now look at you...you a fiend."

Mi-Mi started crying real tears.

I showed her no mercy. Fiend ass bitch. Come up in her frontin' on me. I was ashamed for people to know we were kin.

Liv stopped working on my hair and told me, "That enough, Princess."

Angie said, "Yeah, Princess, leave her alone."

I snapped, "You see this shit, bitch? You got my people up in here feelin' sorry for yo' dusty ass. And you don't even want shit."

I reached under the smock, dug into my Gucci bag, and found a few loose dollars. After I fished them out of my bag, I threw them in Mi-Mi's face. Watching her struggle to catch the crumpled bills before they hit the floor made me shake my head in disgust.

"I knew it," I grumbled. "I knew that was all you wanted. Well...you got you enough for a couple of rocks now. You can get like Michael Jackson and beat it."

Mi-Mi stuffed the bills in her pocket, then she looked up at me all weak and teary-eyed and shit, and said, "You wrong, Princess. And I ain't gon' never forget this shit. I promise you that," she said, then turned and walked away. The ass of her jeans looked like she'd sat in piss or something.

As she walked out the door of the shop, I yelled at her back, "Bitch, please, soon as you smoke that rock you gon' forget everything besides findin' a way to get another one."

Angie said, "Why you do that to Mi-Mi, Princess? That shit was shady as fuck."

Keisha said, "Yeah, bitch, you a shade tree for that shit."

I wasn't tryna to hear that chatter in the background. I hated weak bitches and Mi-Mi was definitely a weak bitch.

I turned to Angie and Kiesha and told them, "I don't fuck with no crack head bitches. If y'all start smokin' that shit, I'm cuttin' y'all asses off, too. Let that be a lesson."

After I said that Angie and Keisha had the nerve to slit their eyes at me.

I don't know why they were tripping? They didn't have anything to worry about unless they were about to start smoking crack.

CHAPTER 21
DONTAE

The sun was shining, but it was still a cold and windy November day when I got down to the 534 building. I pulled the Benz into the back parking lot of the building and found Cat Eyes leaning on his Caddy, A half-empty bottle of Remy sitting on its hood, hotboxing a blunt. Instantly, my mood darkened, it ain't like I was in a good mood in the first place. My head had been fucked up ever since I lost Reggie Wade. I had allowed this shit with him to move into my head and live rent-free, it was like a roommate I couldn't get rid of. I parked, popped out the Benz, and walked over to Cat Eyes. He had that look in his eyes I knew somethin' was wrong. We shook up.

"Cat Eyes, what's up, Jo'?"

"On Fo' nem. That bitch ass, swine ass Faggot Steve been through this bitch hot as a firecracker," Cat Eyes said, then hit his blunt and continued, "He asked me about the shit that happened in the seven-two-seven building."

"What you say?"

Cat Eyes snapped, "Fuck you mean what I say? I ain't say shit, nigga."

"Calm down, Jo."

"You know how I get down. I ain't on no snitch shit."

"I mean, hey," I said holding my hands out in surrender. "I know you ain't tell him shit. If you did, we'd be locked up. I was sayin', period, how the rest of the conversation go?" I said, but it wasn't the truth. I didn't put shit past a nigga in the streets.

You never know where a nigga's breaking point is at. Them is just cold hard facts. A nigga could be solid one time, and straight

148

bitch another time. Circumstances and situations always changed. In the streets, all that mattered was how a nigga held it down during his last test.

Cat Eyes told me about the shit that happened to Lil Tonio. He told me about all the workers ghosting his ass. He was salty about the whole shit.

"So, y'all ain't finish the bundles from yesterday?" I asked, as I leaned on his Caddy and folded my arms.

He blew out air. "You ain't heard a word I said huh, Folks?"

"Yeah," I told him. "I heard you. But whatever happened to, if the people at the front, we move the action to the back? What happened to still don't nothin' move but the money?"

"That shit went out the window for me when Faggot Steve told me to tell you he needed to ask you why he keeps findin' Bomb in a Bag on his murder scenes?"

Cat Eyes let that shit hang in the air.

A couple of cars sped by behind us.

One of them had a fucked-up sound system, but I could hear the bassline of *Ain't No Future In Yo' Frontin'* by Mc Breed. The shit Cat Eyes told me fell and hit me after that. It hit me like ton of bricks.

"He told you to tell me that shit, huh?"

"That's what he told me, Folks."

A brief second passed that felt like an eternity. During that eternity I did some figuring in my head. While I was busy figuring, it dawned on me that Fatso had probably had bundles on him when he was killed. I knew Iroc Tony did 'cause he had copped twenty bundles right before he was killed. It wasn't that much to the shit actually--whether I was responsible for the murder, or not, I'd be a suspect. Dontae Devaughn Kirkpatrick and Bomb in a Bag were the same. Even the little kids in the projects knew that. Reggie Wade was fuckin' me every which way he could.

I told Cat Eyes, "Leave that shit closed. I still got that picture I picked up in seven-two-seven. I'ma holla at Autoboy Arthur for some steamers, Jo'. We need to turn the fire on old boy. You and Sneak meet me back here around ten tonight."

"A'ight, Folks."

Autoboy Arthur was standing out in front of the 511 building when I pulled up and parked on 36th East Browning Street, behind James R. Doolittle Elementary. He was rocking a Bull's Letterman over a black hoodie, jeans, and Jordan twos.

"Tae Murder," Arthur said, showing me all thirty-six of his teeth. "What's up, Famo?"

I walked up on him, shook up with him, and told him, "I need your aid and assist."

"What you on, Famo?"

"I want you to start bringin' me steamers to five-thirty-four every night?"

He looked at me like I had shit on my face. "Famo, ain't you the same nigga who was knockin' my hustle? What happened to steamers causin' undue heat?" he said, then crossed his arm, tilted his head slightly, and waited for an answer. Autoboy Arthur was a little, short nigga, but he was the coldest car thief in the projects. He was so well-known cause if, given the chance, he could peel up a steamer in less than sixty seconds.

"Steamers do cause undue heat, Jo'," I told him. "When you ridin' through here and gettin' into high-speed chases with the law, and shit."

Autoboy Arthur hocked and spit a loogie on the ground. He looked at me crazy as a muhfucka, "What you need the steamers for, Famo?"

I shook my head. "That's a whole other conversation, Jo'," I told him. "You want the job, or not?"

He looked up at the sky, then looked back down at me and said, "Two-fifty a car."

"Two hunnid?"

"One-fifty?"

"One, seventy-five, and I'll have all the gas tanks full?"

We shook up.

"Fair exchange ain't no robbery," I told him.

"It ain't no come up either," Autoboy Arthur said. "I'll park 'em behind your building every night around eight."

"Love, Jo'," I said, then peeled four bills off my money knot for Autoboy Arthur and slapped the bills in his palm. "That's the car', I thought as I walked away from the 511 building, now, I needed to see Pool Hall for the targets.

Later, I knocked on the door of Pool Hall's crib. I got no answer. I could hear the TV on inside. I knew he was home, so I tried the doorknob. It was unlocked, I turned it and walked inside. The air was misty in the place. I smelled liquor and stale cigarettes strong. I walked through the hallway into the living room. Nothin' had changed in Pool Hall's world. I found him on the sofa with his head between his legs, slobbering, nodding, and scratching. Between his first two fingers was a Salem 100, ash down to the filter, hanging on for dear life.

"Bossman, how's it hangin'?" Pool Hall spoke real throaty like he'd just finished screaming at the top of his lungs for an hour. He stayed in his nod, never looked up at me.

"How you know it was me when you nodded out in here like this?" I asked.

"Ain't nobody walkin' up in this muhfucka wearin' Karl Lagerfeld Cologne but you, bossman."

I took a seat on the bucket seat, fished out the photo of the Dirty Snatchers from my pocket, and dropped it on the plywood table.

"Old nigga," I said.

"What I tell you 'bout that shit, bossman?" Pool Hall grumbled as he came out of his nod.

I pointed to the photo on the plywood table and told him, "I need names and whereabouts. I got a sawbuck for each profile you gimmie."

Pool Hall picked the photo up, held it close to his eyes, then held it out like he was trying to focus, cause his eyes were bad. "Lemme get my specs on, bossman." He leaned in on the table and picked up a busted, black eyeglass case. After that, he pulled a pair of bifocals out, blew breath on them, and used the front tail of his blue and white, pinstripe button-up to clean the lenses. Once they were on his face, he began, "Got damn!" he exclaimed. "I ain't seen some of these lousy, low-life muhfuckas in years!"

The first thing I thought about was how Pool Hall who is a stomp-down dope fiend, called other muhfuckas lousy, lowlifes. Then I thought, hell yeah—he recognized all the niggas on the photo. I'm getting somewhere. I needed confirmation.

"Are those the Dirty Snatchers?"

"Live and direct," Pool Hall replied. I could tell the photo took him back to his heydays. He started rubbing his thigh and rocking. "Where you get this picture from?"

"'If I tell you I gotta kill you."

"Never mind, then," Pool Hall said, then leaned in on the table.

I leaned in on the table, too, ignoring his cigarette and liquor breath as he started from the left side of the photo, pointing niggas out and giving me profiles.

Since Bugaloo, Wahmoose, Gypsy, and sky were all dead, and Dirty Bird was locked up, Pool Hall started with all the remaining members of the gang.

Baldy was the stocky one with beady eyes. He had a disease that wouldn't let him grow hair nowhere on his body. He and Stretcher the massive nigga with the dirty dreadlocks to the right of him, was the gang's muscle. Baldy was a dope fiend, but his size had landed him a bouncer gig in the Ritz Lounge. Stretcher was clean now, but he was always in and out of prison, so Pool Hall had no clue where he was. Custom Fit was still playing the *lemme hold somethin, all I find all I keep* game. He had lost most of his weight as of late because he was starting to love crack more than heroin. Another thing was that he'd cut off all his hair and was wearing a short natural now. Pool Hall told me he wouldn't be hard to find. The last nigga was Payne-El, A notorious stick-up man from the rowhouses near the Darrow Homes. He was always dressed in red, black, and green cause he'd been a member of the El-Rukn Nation, an off sho pot of the infamous Black Peace Stones. After the leadership of the El-Rukn was indicted on Federal Rico Conspiracy charges, Payne-El joined the Dirty Snatchers and started takin' money every which way.

"Yeah, but he ain't doin' nothin' now, but smokin' like a broke stove," Pool Hall said as he dropped the photo on the table and fired up a Salem 100. "He stayin' over there with Big Val."

I knew Big Val. Everybody knew Big Val. Valerie Cherry was a 300lb, monster of a bitch, wide as all outside and ugly as a circus freak. She ran a smokehouse out of her rowhouse apartment. I guess she was paying Payne-El to fuck her big nasty ass.

"Bossman, you cleanin' house, huh?" Pool Hall said.

"Keep that under your hat, old nigga."

"I ain't got enough room, bossman."

Just then, I got a call on my cell phone.

"Dontae."

I knew the voice.

It was Angie.

"What up, sis? This me," I said calling her sis to try to create some distance between us.

I was remembering the awkward moment we'd shared the last time we'd seen one another. I had pushed that so far in the back of my mind that I hadn't thought about it since then.

"I need you to stop by here."

I could almost see her tears falling from her eyes on the other side of the line.

"What's wrong?"

"I just need to see you."

"A'ight. Gimme a minute."

I ended the call and after I peeled money off for Pool Hall, I walked out of his crib, headed for Angie's, wondering what was going on with her.

Angie buzzed me in. I walked through the glass and tile lobby and caught the elevator up to her apartment. The door was open. I walked in and locked up behind myself.

"Angie?" I called out as I searched for signs of her.

"I'm back here," she called back to me.

She was crying, I could hear it in her voice. I followed her voice up a hallway, past a bathroom on the left and Rashaun's room on the right. My walk was deliberately slow. A voice was on my right shoulder telling me not to go to her, the voice on my left shoulder was telling me not to be a bitch. In the end, I chose not to be a bitch. I had to go to her. I had come this far. Why would I turn back?

"Sis," I said as I walked even slower. "Where are you?"

"In the bedroom."

The bedroom was at the back of the hallway. The door was cracked. The V-shape shadow on the hallway floor hid from the light. I wanted to go somewhere and hide, too. But I didn't, I just kept it movin' toward the bedroom as uneasy as a kid carrying a switch to his grandmother.

"Turn around, Goofy, don't go in there. You know what's about to happen."

"No, I don't. That's why I wanna go in the room. I'm curious."

"Curiosity killed the cat."

"I heard that before."

I approached the bedroom door, and after ignoring better judgment, I pushed the door into the bedroom.

What I saw paralyzed me. My heart fell to the pit of my stomach like a dead body in Lake Michigan wearing cement shoes. Angie was sitting on the edge of her bed, butt naked, tears falling like rain over her cheeks. A gun was under her chin, both her tiny hands were wrapped around the gun's handle, both her tiny fingers were on the trigger. The hammer was back. The slightest touch of it, and it was good night Irene for her. I looked at the gun. The cannon in her hand was a 9mm Ruger. I recognized that gun. I'd bought it and gave it to Fatso for his last birthday.

I had to get that gun out of her hands. But I knew I couldn't just run up on her and fake it. If I did that, I knew she would pull that trigger, the Ruger would explode, and her melon would open up and all its guts and seeds would eject like an airplane pilot from a falling plane. All I could think about was her pulling that trigger before I got a chance to stop her. If she did that shit I'd never forgive myself.

Shit started moving in slow mo as I took soft steps toward her. "Angie," I almost whispered to her. "Put that gun down. You don't wanna kill yourself."

Her whole body was trembling. Shit! I knew I shouldn't have come over here.

"I'm hurtin' bad, Dontae," she cried. "I'm not goin to be able to live without Fatso. He was my everything. Who gon' want me now? Life just gon' be lonely without him. I ain't got nothin' to live for."

"You know that ain't true, Angie," I told her as I crept toward her, still in slow-mo. "What about Rashaun, Angie? Your son Rashaun? Fatso's son Rashaun! What about him?" I had her attention. I just had to keep this going. "He already lost his daddy. How you think he gon' take losin' his momma, too?" After I said that another scary moment passed, then Angie broke down. She moved the gun away from her chin. I lunged at her and slapped it out of her hands.

It hit the floor.

Poc!

I swooped over to it, picked it up, ejected the clip, and put it in my pocket. At that moment my heart floated back to the top of my stomach.

"Angie," I said sitting down beside her and throwing my arm around her as she cried into her palms. "When I was in the Audy Home, some years back, this Spanish boy hung himself from the light in his cell. After he did that shit, they bought a counselor in there to talk to us, and he told us suicide is a permanent solution to temporary problems. Whatever you're goin' through right now, you ain't gon' go through that shit forever."

Angie sat up straight and fell into me. "I know it might seem like you ain't gon' ever get over Fatso, sis. But you will and Fatso would want you to."

"I don't know, Dontae," she cried. "It just hurts so bad. All I do is think about him. I can't get him off my mind. Every time I try, his memory just comes right back to haunt me. That's why I sent Rashaun to my momma's house. I can't look at his face. He reminds me of his dad."

I let her talk through her pain as I held her, my dead homie's baby momma. She was naked and soft under me, smelling like exotic fruits. She had bathed, she had oiled her skin. Her hair was perfect, her mani-pedi, was on point like an icepick. For a moment, I wondered why she had got so fly to die. Then, I thought maybe she wanted to leave a beautiful corpse.

Suddenly, she looked up at me with those pretty ass eyes and hypnotized me. The moment we shared this time was even more awkward than the awkward moment we'd shared before.

She told me, "Dontae, I can't live like this. I need to get Fatso off my mind." She placed a hand on my thigh.

I asked, "Angie, what you doin'?"

"Come on, Dontae," she said. "I saw how you looked at me last time you came here."

I knew what she had seen in my eyes. But I didn't know if she was comfortable enough to speak on that shit. I knew I wasn't.

"Help me forget about him, Dontae?" Angie said as she moved her hand higher up my thigh.

I knew I should've stopped her, but I didn't. My dick was gettin' hard.

"Please, Dontae?" she begged. "I'm hurtin', I'm hurtin' so bad. I just wanna forget him. Please," she said as she squeezed my hard dick through my pants.

The material of my sweats let her grab me like she wanted to. She massaged me good.

"Help me make the pain stop," she said, then kissed me with a lot of wet tongue and a lot of watermelon lip gloss.

I kissed her back and that shit tasted like a mouth full of watermelon jolly ranchers.

The break was mutual.

I told her, "Angie, this shit wrong. You know we bogus."

She rolled her eyes, sighed, and whined, "I know...I know, Dontae. I know this is wrong. But right now, I just wanna feel better. Dontae, help me feel better. Just this one time. I swear to God, I'll never say nothin' to Princess about it. My shit is just all messed up right now. I just need you to fuck me."

"You just need me to fuck you, huh?"

"Just this one time," she said. "You ain't gotta make love. Just need you to fuck me."

After I heard her say that all my morals and principles went on the window. I stood up and undressed. She helped me match her nakedness with my own. In record time, she had my hard dick in her hands sucking it like a hungry baby. Her tears never stopped falling over her dimpled cheeks. As she sucked me good, I convinced myself I wasn't betraying my nigga Fatso. All I was doin' was helping one friend get over another one. I told myself whatever I needed to tell myself to keep me from feeling guilty.

All of sudden, Angie stopped sucking my dick and looked at me. Her eyes were red and puffy. Her whole face was drenched in tears.

I gazed down at her, all pretty and petite titties, nipples were hard and perky. She was a bad lil muhfucka. But she didn't belong to me, she belonged to Fatso.

Or did she?

She held onto my hard dick, tugging on it, using it to pull me along as she scooted back onto the bed. All the while, her eyes never left mine.

"Come on, Dontae?" she cried. "I want you to fuck me until I can't think about nothin' else but bein' fucked." She spread her legs.

I climbed on top of her. I broke through the wet lips of her clean-shaven pussy and pounded her walls like a dime bag dope date. I didn't know if I could help her with her pain. I didn't know if I could keep her from tryna commit suicide again. But what I did know was she would forget about Fatso. At least she'd forget about him while I was up in her.

CHAPTER 22

CAT EYES

"Uh-uh, nigga! Where you goin'?"

That was Kiesha. She was tripping a-fuckin-gain cause I was leaving. I looked at my watch, it was fifteen to ten. I needed to get to the building to meet Dontae, and I hadn't even stopped by to scoop Sneak, yet. This bitch was bout to have me late with her bullshit.

I spun around and told her, "I gotta get outta here, Kee-Kee."

The bitch said, "Where you gotta go, Cat Eyes, huh? Where you gotta go?" she snapped as she leaped off the bed and ran up on me like she wanted the business. "You gotta go do somethin' for Dontae? You ain't even gotta say it. I know what it is. One night, I asked you to stay in and watch a movie with me and your son, and you can't even do that."

"You tweakin', Kee-Kee," I told her, as I put a hand on my forehead and brought it down over my face. "I'm comin' right back. I just gotta handle somethin'."

"Comin right back my ass, nigga. The last time you told me you was comin' right back, you ain't come back for two days. I know what it is. It gotta be Dontae. Whenever Dontae asks you to jump you don't do nothin' but ask him how high. You act like y'all fuckin' or somethin'!"

"Watch yo' muhfuckin' mouth fo' I stick a fist in it!" I snapped. "Don't you ever disrespect me like that again!"

She piped down. "I'm just sayin'...I don't see him jumpin' up, leavin' Princess every time you call on him. And I bet he wouldn't, I know he wouldn't."

"You need to shut yo' ass up, Kee-Kee," I told her. "You don't know shit."

"Oh, I know more than you think I know. I know you been runnin' that dope line for Dontae for years now and you ain't got shit to show for it. You still drivin' that same raggedy-ass Cadillac while that nigga Dontae ridin' around in a brand-new Mercedes Benz. He and Princess got a plush ass condo off the lake, me, you, and Kalen is still livin' in The Wells in this lil' ass room in my momma's crib. I was with Princess earlier and she took me and Angie shoppin' and to get our hair done. That bitch is drivin' a brand-new BMW. When we was shoppin', she was swipin' all kinds of cards. Ain't neither one of us got no credit cards. Baby, are you that blind, you can't see what's goin' on?"

"Ain't nothin' goin' on, Kee-Kee," I told her, but in my heart, I knew she was right.

"Yes, it is, baby. And you know it. He treatin' you like a flunkie," she said, then got closer to me, threw her arms around my neck, and looked up into my eyes. "Fatso died out there and left Angie with Rashaun. He lost his life and the man ain't have nothin' to show for it. I just don't want you to leave me and Kalen like that."

"I ain't gon' leave y'all like that."

"How can you be sure of that?"

I thought about her question for a moment, and she was right, I couldn't be sure of that. Niggas died every day out in the streets and a lotta muhfuckas lost their lives for nothing.

"I'm doin' what I gotta do, right now, Kee-Kee," I told her. "I'ma get my turn soon."

She just looked at me skeptically. She had a right to not believe me. I hadn't come through for us in all this time. Why should she believe I'd come through in the future? I looked around the bedroom. Her bed was queen-sized, her closet was full of our designer. This was all of my world, I had to do better than this. I needed to start playing for keeps.

"You can't wait for a nigga to give you a turn, baby," Kiesha told me. "You gotta take it,"

I listened to her cause she was telling me some real shit. I just wasn't feeling the fact that I'd had to hear this shit from my baby momma. But who else was I gonna hear it from?

After all, we'd met when we were nine years old. She knew me better than anybody else. She knew me even better than I knew myself sometimes. I couldn't knock her for wanting better for us. I wanted better for us, too.

"Kee-Kee, we gon' be straight," I told her. "Just gimme a lil' more time and I'ma come up on some loot, I'ma get us new cars and I'ma get us a beautiful two-bedroom condo somewhere classy."

"Make that condo a three-bedroom."

"Why would I do that when it's just me, you, and Kalen?"

"It won't be just me, you and Kalen that much longer," she said, then she cocked her head to the side, smiled, and rubbed her belly in a circle. "I'm pregnant!"

CHAPTER 23
REGGIE WADE

"I can't fuck with that mog Reggie Wade, Jo'. That nigga scurvy as a muhfucka."

"I ain't sayin' we should fuck with him. I'm just sayin' buy the bundles from him. Cause he sellin' 'em for the low."

"I don't know, Jo'. That mog fuck around and sell us that shit and try to double back and rob a muhfucka."

I didn't know why I was fuckin' with these young, dumb-ass, scary-ass niggas. Most of the time these young muhfuckas ain't know they assholes from a hole in the ground. First of all, a little young nigga I knew, by the name of Scooter had walked me into the dope house of one of his GD brothers. I guess he was under the assumption that I wouldn't front him off, by pulling a stick-up while I was with him. Truthfully, I wasn't on that shit. I just wanted to sell some of the bundles I'd come up on lately and put together a bankroll for Mi-Mi cause, earlier today she had come to my crib in tears talking about how bad her cousin had treated her. She hadn't said much more than that, but I knew whatever was said, had broken her down emotionally, and dealt a crushing blow to her self-esteem. After I'd talked to her about that shit, she'd asked me for scratch to get her glamor together. I told her I had her. Why not? I was starting to dig on the punk bitch.

So, that's what had brought me over to The Backyard section of The Wells. Where I was standing in an empty rowhouse apartment, that was nothing but a cleaned-out vaco with burglar bars on the front and back doors. While Scooter was in the bedroom tryna convince his man, Petty Mark did they not know how thin the project walls were. That's why I don't know why I was fucking with these young, dumb-ass, scary-ass niggas.

"My uncle told me that nigga's always on some stick-up shit, Folks. He just be poppin' up on muhfuckas, no car, or nothin'. Why you bring that nigga to my spot?"

"You straight, Jo'. He ain't on that shit. That nigga got ten fifty packs of Bomb in a Bag. All he wants for them bitches is five hunnid a bundle. You know Bomb in a Bag got a nuke on the boy. All you gotta do is buy the bundles and put them muhfuckas in yo' seals and you double yo' money. The shit gon' fly like hotcakes."

"It sounds sweet, Jo'. On the real, I just don't trust that mog."

"Folks, he ain't gon' stick you up. I know the nigga. His grandmother used to babysit me when I was a shorty. His ole G and my ole G was friends."

"Fuck that 'posed to mean?"

"It means he ain't gon' get on that with us, like he on that with them niggas in the body bags."

"You green as the White House lawn, Jo'. That nigga ain't got no cut cards. He'll probably do his own mother."

I listened to the young nigga's logic of this street shit and he was actually on point. Only, I hadn't come with robbery intentions tonight. But the way this muhfucka was holding me up with his hoe shit was pissing me the fuck off.

Scooter came walking out of the bedroom with his head down. His dark face had an expression on it that said he had to take a mean shit. He zipped up his Buffalo Bills Starter coat, adjusted the matching skull cap on his afro. His body language showed defeat.

He told me, "He ain't tryna fuck with you, Jo'. He basically sayin' you too shiesty."

Petty Mark walked out of the bedroom. He was a slim nigga with an overbite. He was wearing a black Carhart overall, and he appeared heavy under it. "Mack buddy," he said clapping his hands together. "No disrespect, mellow, cause I don't know you. But I heard a lil' bit about you in the streets and wasn't none of that shit good. You feel me? Plus, that's Dontae 'nem shit you tryna sell me. If it ever came out that I grabbed some of his shit from you, I can get brought on charges and the Folks, definitely give a muhfucka a pumpkin head for that shit. So—"

"You know what, shorty," I told him. "I woulda respected the shit you just told me, if I hadn't just heard you in the room bad mouthin' me, and shit. On ehthang, I came here to do good business, but since you think a muhfucka on some bullshit, I'ma get on that with you," I said, as I swung The Beast up 'till its barrel was in the young nigga's chest. "Don't bip to bop, muhfucka. If you do, I'll make this bitch huff and puff and blow yo' bitch ass down," I growled. "Now, gimmie everything in this muhfucka?"

In my peripheral vision, I could see Scooter easing toward the front door.

"Damn, Scooter, G!" Petty Mark snapped. "You set me up, Folks! You bogus as a muhfucka!"

"I ain't set you up, G—"

I barked on Scooter, "Scoot get yo' stupid ass over here and find somethin' to tie this bitch ass nigga up with!"

"Reggie, come on, Jo'," Scooter begged. "Don't do this shit, it's on my face."

"Blood gon' be on yo' face if you don't listen to me, vic!" I snapped. "You might as well help me now. Cause you a cooked duck. You heard this bitch as nigga. He thinks you set him up."

It didn't take Scooter a long time to realize he was better off helping me than just standing around watching. He ransacked the apartment and came back into the living room with what appeared to be a little girl's double-dutch jump rope and started tying Petty Mark's wrists together.

"Scooter, you a bitch ass nigga for tha shit!"

I held The Beast on Petty Mark as Scooter tied him down tight. Just then, I heard a solid knock at the door.

I answered like the spot was mine, "Who that?"

"Y'all workin', shorty?"

Right then and there I remembered that Petty Mark was running his heroin out of the crib. I told the knocker at the door, "Five minutes." I turned my attention back to Petty Mark.

"Where that dope and that scratch at, nigga?"

Scooter told me, "He keeps the dope behind the refrigerator, and the scratch in the bottom of the dirty clothes bag, in the bedroom closet."

"If you already know where that shit at," I told Scooter. "Go get that shit and bring it in here."

Scooter left the living room, and suddenly I heard metal being scooted back and forth across tiles.

I looked at Petty Mark. He had a sick look on his face.

I told him, "I was about to play fair with you on some palms up shit, shorty, but you made me play for keeps."

There was another knock on the door. I didn't respond this time. After that, Scooter came back into the living room with a heavy, white pillowcase, He tried to hand it to me.

I told him, "Nall, you hold on to it." After I told him that, I pulled a Desert Eagle out of my waist and held it out toward Scooter. "Take this heat and blow this nigga shit out."

Scooter hesitated for a moment, then he grabbed the heat from me and aimed it at Petty Mark's face.

Petty Mark braced himself. "No!" he screamed.

Boom!

The Desert Eagle exploded with a burst of orange flame that cracked Petty Mark's skull and busted out of the back of his head. At the same time, a red mist hallowed over him and brains and blood sounded like paint splashing on plastic. The nigga curled up in the fetal, convulsed, and bled out. I pulled out a Bomb in a Bag bundle. Busted the baggie open and shook it out on the floor around Petty Mark.

After that, I told Scooter, "Let's get in the wind, shorty."

Scooter moved my way. I looked out the front window, saw muhfuckas standing in front of the building, and said, "We can't go out the front, shorty. Look out the back window and see if anybody's back there."

"Aight," he said, then turned around.

Before he could put his right foot down in front of his left.

Boom!

I pulled the trigger of The Beast. The slug blasted through his back and made him do a somersault. His intestines splattered all over the floor. I walked up on him, squatted down, and pried the Desert Eagle and the pillowcase from his fingers as he gurgled and choked on his own blood.

I lived by a motto: The lone wolf ain't gotta share his kill.

CHAPTER 24
DONTAE

The Ritz Hotel was a raunchy joint on the corner of Muddy Waters Boulevard and King Drive. It was one those joints whores took tricks, up and coming crack dealers opened shop, and old stick-up niggas hid out after stains and got high. You didn't get asked for it at The Ritz. You were never asked any questions. All they expected you to do was pay by the hour, and in return, you got a small room with cum stains on the sheets. Cigarette burns on the furniture and in the carpet, bullet holes in the walls, and all the privacy that thin shell could offer—which wasn't much. The lounge behind The Ritz was just raunchy. It was nothing but a hole-in-the-wall that wasn't there at all to most muhfuckas. A crop of thick bushes aided the wooden, slat fence that accessed the joint. Behind the fence, there was a window cement path that led to a staircase that climbed up a couple of flights and spit a nigga out in front of a steel door.

Like I said: It wasn't there at all to most muhfuckas.

It was after 11:00 p.m. when I pulled up on the King Drive's service drive and parked in front of the lounge and storefront on 40th Street. The sky was pitch black. The hawk was out. Condensation was floating up out of manholes. It was fall in the windy quiet and fall in the windy city was nothing but winters in a ski mask and gloves.

The steamer Autoboy Arthur had brought me and a black-on-black 69 Nova with pipes and words the tires. That muhfucka had some shit under the hood that could get a nigga outta any jam. Too bad I had to burn it after the move.

As I sat behind the wheel with the photo of the Dirty Snatchers in my hand, Cat Eyes turned toward me in the passenger seat. Sneak threw his arms and chest over the front seat. I pointed

Baldy out to them, and they nodded with understanding. After that, we sat back and settled in for the wait.

Baldy was a bouncer in The Ritz lounge, he had to show his face at some point.

I scanned the scene. The usual crack heads and dope heads chased their high up and down the strip. The traffic out on the main boulevard was light compared to most nights. The El-train wasn't clattering up the tracks a couple of blocks West.

Cat Eyes fired up a blunt. "You know what, Folks," he said with a look of seriousness on his face that bothered me. "I needed to holla at you about somethin' later."

"What you on, Jo'?" I asked tryna pry the shit out of him.

"It's personal, Folks," he told me. "We need to holla, though."

"A'ight."

Now I was wondering what was on Cat Eyes's mind. It had to be something serious because he'd brought that shit up, right in the middle of us bussing a move. The Angie situation was still a category F5 tornado on my mind. I was already dealing with finding the loose cannon that had robbed me and killed Fatso. I didn't need some more shit coming outta left field.

I sat there smoking with Cat Eyes and Sneak. The hours passed like a slick nigga on the dice. When I looked at my watch it was ten to 2:00 a.m. Sneak was in the back seat restless as hell. Cat Eyes was nodding in and out. I was about to call it a night. When I spotted Baldy.

"Sneak," I said, on ten and pointing at the dark, bulky nigga with no facial hair, period. "That's him, Jo'."

Sneak looked at the nigga and the look that crossed his grill reminded me of a ferocious pit bull.

Baldy was wearing a pea coat and beads of sweat was all over his bald head. Steam rose from his body. Obviously, he'd been in a warm space getting high.

Cat Eyes opened the passenger door and Sneak squeezed out.

Sneak stepped out on the curb backward, capping at us, "The bitch told me she was gon' be up here after the spot closed. It's closed now. I'ma see if she's comin' out."

He bumped into Baldy.

Baldy pushed him away and said, "Youngster, where you goin'."

Sneak said, "Oh, shit! My bad, OG."

When Baldy, spun off, Sneak upped his 9mm Glock, aimed it at the back of Baldy's head, and pulled the trigger.

Blatt! The bullet hit Baldy square in the back of his bald head and knocked a patch out of it.

His neck snapped forward and bloody, red mist sprayed the air before he tumbled. Forward and fell on his face. Once he hit the ground, Sneak stood over him and fired two more shots in his melon.

Blatt! Blatt!

The shots splattered his brains all over the pavement as dope fiends screamed and scattered.

I opened my door, crawled out of the steamer, and screamed, "Somebody tell Reggie Wade his ass gotta pay for that bullshit he did at the five-thirty-four building!"

I looked down at Baldy as Sneak ran back over to the steamer and squeezed into the back seat. That nigga's shit was caved in. His shit looked like cherry pie. Sneak had definitely bussed the nigga shit. It was over for him.

I jumped back into the steamer and pulled away from the mayhem in no hurry. Sneak was geeked up in the back seat.

"You see how I just opened that nigga's shit up, G! That work right there was classic! A muhfucka gon' remember that shit, right there!"

Cat Eyes asked me, "Who's next, Folks?"

I told him, 'Custom Fit."

Cat Eyes rubbed his palms together and smiled like a Cheshire cat. "Yeah, I'ma custom fit his ass for a casket."

CHAPTER 25
ANGIE

I never had any intentions of killing myself. Come on, a pretty bitch like me. Never! I just wanted Dontae to fuck me, and I knew he wouldn't have done that shit if I just asked him. He wasn't the kind of nigga who went around dirty-dicking every female that winked and smiled at him. He definitely wasn't the kinda nigga that would start fucking his homie's baby momma not even a whole month after he'd been killed. But I needed him to be that nigga for me. The fake suicide attempt was supposed to turn him into that nigga and that shit had worked. My pussy was still sore from the pounding he'd put on me. I loved the way he'd put it down. I'd cum so many times that I forgot to count. I don't remember Fatso ever fucking me like Dontae had. That nigga got himself a bomb on the dick.

I know y'all judging me now cause Princess is supposed to be my friend, but fuck that. Y'all saw how shady that bitch is. Any woman with that kinda heart don't need a real nigga like Dontae in her life. The shit she did to Mi-Mi gave me all the excuse I needed to cross her stankin' ass. As if that wasn't enough, she had the nerve to tell me and Keisha that she would treat us the same way. The fuck! I shoulda checked the bitch right then and there, for real for real, but I kept my composure. It was always more than one way to skin cat. Princess was a cat that needed a real good skinning.

"Baby, that bitch Mi-Mi's better than me. Cause if she woulda popped slick outta her mouth like that to me, I woulda drug that bitch all through that shop." That was Keisha.

She called me this morning to talk to me about Princess's shady ass. I had just gotten out of the tub and oiled my skin when I got her call. Now, I was sitting in my bedroom in my white lace panties and bra, talking on the phone with her. She was giving me an ear full.

"You know I really don't fuck with her for real, anyways. You know she thinks she better than us. And remember that shit she did when we all went to the Sybirus for Dontae's birthday?"

I definitely remembered that shit. Princess had gotten naked and gotten into the Jacuzzi with Cat Eyes before everybody else had come into the room. Kiesha was salty. I had to talk her out of dog walking Princess's ass.

"She thinks cause she's Dontae main bitch she some kinda boss or somethin'. I don't see how you fuck with that bitch. You are so much better than that," Keisha said.

I thought about Princess for a moment. We'd been tight since grade school. She'd always been a little bossy, but for real for real, she had never been so bougie.

I told Keisha, "She wasn't always like she is now. Ever since she started fuckin' with Dontae she don' became a whole other person."

"I guess you don't know people until they got money."

"I guess you're right about that."

Dontae deserves so much better than Princess. Only if he knew who she really was. Out of respect for the girl code, I'd held onto all her secrets, all her lies, and betrayals. In part, because she'd held onto mine. But now that she'd become Queen Isabella I was thinking about ways to bring Tina Topnotch down a few pegs.

Keisha said, "She really treated Mi-Mi bad, girl. Didn't she?"

"Yeah," I said agreeing with Keisha wholeheartedly. "She did."

"My momma smoke's crack, Angie," Keisha admitted hurtfully. "She's been strugglin' with that addiction for years now. But I'd never talk to her like Princess talked to Mi-Mi."

Keisha was a strong, young woman who had gone through a lot at a very young age cause of her mother's addiction. She had to boost and have sex with dope dealers for money to feed herself and her siblings cause her mother would spend all the welfare and Food stamps on crack. Princess knew this about Keisha and that's why she always tried low-key act like Keisha was beneath her. What I didn't understand about Princess was why she believed she was better than Keisha. When her father had died of a heroin overdose. Keisha was from The Wells and me and Princess were from the two complexes on either side of the projects, but we all had attended the same schools, shopped at the same stores, and lived in the same neighborhood. Princess needed to step down off her high horse. Now, that I thought about what she'd did to Mi-Mi I understood the method of her madness. Mi-Mi reminded her that she was no different than any other bitch in that shop.

"Before Mi-Mi got strung-out she was about that action too, girl," I said. "If Mi-Mi wasn't high and fucked up on them drugs, she probably woulda beat Princess's ass."

"Ain't no probably to it."

That bitch Mi-Mi had hands. She had been the one always taking up for Princess whenever she had let her mouth overload her ass. The thing about Princess was that she was all talk. She had been that way ever since we were kids.

"Anyways," Keisha said. "I can do a whole talk show on Princess's ass. What's up with you, girl? Did you find that dick you needed?"

"I did actually."

"I knew it," Keisha blurted. "I could tell, cause you wasn't soundin' all depressed and shit."

"Get outta here, girl, ain't nobody been depressed. I was just grievin', Keisha. I lost my son's father. It's a lotta shit goin' on in my head."

"Yeah, yeah, yeah. I hear you. But enough about that, bitch. Let's talk about that dick you sucked last night."

"Look at your nasty ass. I bet you would wanna talk about that."

"Is he anybody I know?"

"As a matter of fact, he is."

"Well?"
"Well, what?"
"Well, spit it out, bitch. Who is he?"

CHAPTER 26
DETECTIVE STEVEN KNOX

I showed up at the rowhouse building where two young, black, males were found in a vacant apartment dead. They'd both been shot, one with a large caliber handgun, and the other with a shotgun. I would've figured the shooting was random. I had found more Bomb in a Bag dope bags on the scene. Somebody was deliberately placing these bags around dead building. The shit was starting to piss me off now. Normally, I kept my emotions out of a case, but I knew something was going on between Dontae and Reggie Wade. This is where me and the law always came in conflict. I needed evidence and witnesses to charge a suspect, and this little chink in the law armor allowed bad people to continue doing bad things. Luckily, I had other ways of dealing with bad people. I just had to find them.

I walked out of the building into the fall, leaves were all over the ground. They crunched under my boots as I walked back to the box.

"Steve!"

I heard my name and turned around. Jill was walking toward me, no make-up, hair in a tight ponytail, leather, jeans, and Nike cross-trainers. I sized her up, top-heavy, bottom heavier. I wanted some of that pussy and the bitch knew it. That's why she was playing hard to get, but that was alright with me. When I got my chance I'd play for keeps. Traffic zipped North and South on Vincennes and East and West on 37th Place as Jill finally stopped in front of me.

She stuck her hands in the pockets of her jacket, smiled, and told me, "I wanna thank you again for the dinner. I also wanted to apologize for having to run in the middle of it. It's just—"

"No need to explain," I told her. "It was nothin'."

That was bullshit. The bitch had eaten and ran on me before I'd gotten a chance to make my move. If we had been somewhere like Ronny's Steakhouse I wouldn't't've given a fuck, but she'd tricked me to a Five-Star restaurant in Old Town. That bill had cost me half a month's salary, Jill had better have golden pussy lips, a real pearl tongue, and cum that tasted like Pralines and cream.

"I like you, Steve," she told me. "But I just got out of a relationship. You're gonna have to be a little patient with me if you wanna get to know me a little better."

I wasn't a damn fool. I knew the bitch was telling me I had to wait for the pussy. I wasn't used to having patience when it comes to sex. I had an animalistic sex drive that had to be tended to.

I told her, "I don't have a problem being patient with you, Jill. I really like you, too. But I'm a man, you know? I have certain needs that have to be fulfilled."

"I know," she said as she nodded. "I'm not askin' you to be patient alone. You don't owe me that. What you do owe me is respect. I'll work with you on the rest later."

I smiled at her. She smiled and ran her tongue around in her mouth. I don't know who this bitch thought she was playing with, but she'd learn soon enough.

"You'll work with me, huh?" I asked.

She nodded. "Yes, all you men need to be worked with. But don't worry, I'll be just as patient with you as you are with me," she said, then she turned and sashayed away.

I only had a few moments of headspace to dedicate to her, I began thinking about the two extra bodies that someone had just added to my caseload. I could be patient with a nice piece of ass, it was the murders that were trying my patience.

CHAPTER 27
DONTAE

The sky looked like blotches of blood on cement when me, Cat Eyes and Sneak hopped into another steamer, a black Pontiac Firebird, and started hitting blocks.

"Custom Fit be in the zone, Jo'," I told Sneak and Cat Eyes. "I'ma just circle until we see him. Bet?"

"That's a bet," Cat Eyes said as he nodded his head, zoning out to Above *The Law's Sons Of Murder* rap.

He had his black ski mask rolled up on his forehead. His 9mm Glock was in his lap. He was ready to buss a nigga's shit. I hit the block at Vernon Avenue, keeping my eyes peeled for any sign of Custom Fit. Custom Fit was a helluva name, he'd gotten it because he was a hood tailor, airbrushing shirts, jeans, and shoes and shit. That was before the crack. After getting hooked on the glass dick he'd started sticking up. His first hustle was what he shoulda stuck with. Cause his new hustle was about to get him custom fitted for a suit and a coffin.

After an hour of hitting the blocks, we'd finally spotted Custom Fit. He was standing in front of one of the four-story low rises in The Zone section of the projects. He was wearing a plaid wool coat with fur around the hood, fatigue pants, and suede boots he'd been released from prison in.

"That's him in the plaid coat," I told Cat Eyes.

He told me, "I see him. Lemme out on the corner. I'll meet y'all on the service drive." I dropped Cateyes off at the corner of 39th and Vernon. The strip was packed. Dope fiends were still shouting the names of Heroin bags.

"Thunder!"

"Famous!"

"Twenty Paid!"

I pressed the gas and took the steamer West on 39th Street past Nevada Liquor, past Atlanta Foods, and before I bent a right and came up on the service I heard.

Blocka! Blocka! Blocka! There was a short pause in between the first volley shots, then, *Blocka! Blocka! Blocka! Blocka! Blocka!*

When I pulled to a slow stop I saw Cat Eyes standing over Custom Fit. I saw everybody scattering and finding something better to do.

Blocka! Blocka! Blocka! All melon shots.

From the car, I could see Cat Eyes kick Custom Fit a couple of times. After that, he squatted over him and touched him.

I hopped out of the car and shouted, "Bring yo' ass on, nigga!"

Cat Eyes snapped out of whatever kinda murderous trance he was in. Then he ran over to the steamer and hopped into the passenger seat. I hopped in behind the wheel and pulled away.

"What the fuck was that shit, G?" Sneak asked him.

I said, "Yeah, what the fuck was that?"

Cat Eyes' two upper fangs were much larger than the rest of his teeth so when he smiled, he looked more sinister than happy. "Y'all lived that shit, huh? I saw that shit in a movie. I was chockin' to see if the nigga was dead."

I shook my head.

Sneak laughed.

"Who we got next, G?" Sneak asked.

I told him, "Payne-El."

The following night the steamer was a black iroc Z28 Camaro. It looked like a car nigga's killed in. It was low and squatted, and when the headlights were turned out, it crept through the streets like a beetle in the dark. It was dusted fast enough to get ghost if necessary. The traffic on 39th Street was petering out and when pulled into the filler station beside the grimy, Zanzibar motel.

The Zanzi was another one of those pay-by-hour-joints where nothing good went on. You didn't get caught dead there, or you got found dead there. Coming up it had been my kinda spot.

I pulled up in front of the filler station and stopped in front of its glass door as muhfuckas came stumbling out.

"Sneak," I said, turning toward him in the back seat. "Go in there and grab some lighter fluid, and a couple of towels, Jo'." I turned to Cat Eyes in the front seat. "You go grab a six-pack of beer. I'll meet y'all on the block with the two, orange poles," I told them I'd meet them on that block, which was the first block off 39th Street, cause I didn't want to draw attention in the steamer before the move. Ever since the first night of our purge, the law had been scorching hot. They were down over-lapping patrols up and down the stripped.

Cat Eyes and Sneak took turns hopping out of the steamer, and as soon as their feet hit the ground, I whipped out of the filler station, bent a hard left on Rhodes Street, another hard right on 30th Place, and parked in a space behind a broken-down navy Ford Tempo. An old man went riding by on a red bike. A mangy, black terrier trotted alongside him as he disappeared into a courtyard.

A few moments later, Cat Eyes and Sneak came jogging around the corner and hopped into the steamer.

"Y'all grab all that shit?" I asked.

"Drive, Folks," Cat Eyes told me flatly.

I started the steamer, hit the gas, and whipped us over to the 600 block of East 38th Street. A flock of females in starter coats, tight jeans, and gym shoes was walking up the block. The females were a gang. Everybody was in a gang here. The world as we knew always forced a muhfucka to put his or her back up against somebody else's.

I said, "Sneak, there go yo' piece, Tasha."

Sneak snapped, "I don't fuck with that car booty ass bitch."

Cat Eyes told him, "You frontin' like a muhfucka, Jo'. You was just in the seven-two-seven building riskin' yo' life to fuck that lil' bitch."

Sneak said, "Get the fuck outta here."

That was his way of accepting defeat.

Tasha walked by the steamer, spotted Sneak in the back seat, smiled, and waved but kept it pushing.

Sneak dropped his head.

I waited until the females crossed Langley Street before I got to the business at hand.

"Sneak," I said. "You gotta go in and see if the mog Payne-El in there."

"Why I gotta be the one to do it?" Sneak protested.

"Cause it can't be me or Eyes, Jo'," I told him. "You know why."

Me and Cat Eyes already had a reputation for bussin' a nigga's shit. Whenever we were out lurking at night muhfuckas stayed out of our way.

Sneak squeezed out of the back seat, crawled out the steamer, and jogged into the rowhouse building of Big Val smokehouse. He was gone for every bit of five minutes before he came jogging back out of the building and back to the steamer. He came around to my window. I lowered it and he leaned on the frame.

"That nigga in there, G," he said.

I hopped out of the steamer. Cat Eyes hopped out of the passenger door with the bags. After that, I led him and Sneak to a hallway in the dark courtyard behind Big Val's rowhouse building.

The hallway was dark, dank, and full of trash. I found a space on the floor and began making Molotov cocktails out of the materials Cat Eyes and Sneak had bought.

Imitate and emulate, monkey see monkey do, this is how niggas learned the game. In that vein, Cat Eyes and Sneak helped me put together enough Molotov's to burn down the entire building. Big Val already had a smokehouse: may as well be some fire in there, too.

I handed Cat Eyes three of the Molotov's while I took the other three. "You got the back, Jo'. Just aim at Big Val's windows. I'll do the front. If Payne-El runs out the back, buss his shit. You already know what I'ma do if he runs out the front," I said, then I turned to Sneak. "Start the steamer."

Sneak took off as me and Cat Eyes skulled around the rowhouse building to take out positions. The plan was to throw the Molotov's through the window of Val's crib and cause a big enough fire to make everyone inside come running outside. This was the plan.

I sat the Molotov's on the ground in front of me, lit them one at a time, then I threw each of them at the windows of Big Val's crib. The first Molotov cracked the living room window bounced off and fell beside the building in ablaze. I threw the second, and the third and both crashed through the windows. In seconds, I could hear the hot breath of fire, and I could see the orange blaze licking the air outside the window like a lizard tongue. Screams bellowed out from inside Big Val's crib. All of a sudden, paranoid crack heads came trampling and stampeding over one another as they fought their way out of the hallway door. A few of them stopped, dropped, and rolled, while others took off running full speed up the street with their clothes on fire. I crept up beside the hallway just in time to catch Payne-El run out. He was sweating profusely, his eyes were big as pie saucers and he was barefooted. He gazed around in confusion. He had no idea it was his night to die. I upped Fatso's Ruger on him.

Shock froze him like Simon says.

Blocka!

The slug burst out of the barrel of the Ruger with an orange tail. All that shit slammed into Payne-El's chest. He did a slight jumping jack and a sound escaped him that came from his gut. I aimed the Ruger higher until the barrel was pointed at his melon.

Blocka!

I pulled the trigger, and that slug bussed his shit. He crumpled to the pavement and hit it like a sandbag. Just then, Cat Eyes came running around the building, and we stood over Payne-El.

Blocka! Blocka! Blocka! Blocka! Blocka! Blocka! Blocka!

We emptied our clips as Sneak rolled up beside us in the steamer. Behind the entire building was a raging blaze of orange and blue flames.

I scowled and spun in a slow circle with the smoking Ruger at my thigh and shouted for the world to hear, "If you stickin' up in The Wells it ain't safe for you out here! I got enough guns and bullets. I'll kill until blood floods the drains around this muhfucka! Somebody tell that bitch ass nigga Reggie Wade he's the next nigga to get his ass bussed."

CHAPTER 28
REGGIE WADE

"Law Enforcement are investigating a sudden uptick in gun violence in the Ida B. Wells Housing Projects, on Chicago's Lower Southside. Investigators say there's been a string of homicides they believe are connected to the robbery-homicide of Quincy Fatso Moore, a resident of the 600 Block of East 37th Street, whose shooting occurred a month ago in the lobby of a building at 534 East 37th Street. Quincy Fatso Moore was found dead from a single gunshot wound to the chest, and in the subsequent weeks that followed his shooting. There have been multiple homicides that culminated last night with a grisly, brazen attack on the rowhouse building at 630 East 30th Street. A witness says, a black Camaro Z28, pulled up in front of the building, just before midnight, and threw Molotov cocktails into a second-floor apartment, the assailants then laid wait outside, until Walter Payne-El appeared running out of the building.

The assailants opened fire on the victim, and afterward, they jumped back into the vehicle and sped away from the scene. The vehicle the assailants were riding in was later found on fire beside a vacant lot on Calumet Avenue. The vehicle had been reported stolen on November 2nd, 1991—in other news—"

I rolled out of bed early to get some dope in me. I needed to chase the hawks away before I was able to deal with the world as it was being presented to me. In the last three days Baldy, Custom Fit, and Payne-El had all had their shit split. Not to mention my old running buddy, Sky Davis. He had caught a bad one, been shot, and tossed out of the 6th Floor window of his own crib. Dontae deserved my undivided attention. He had proved this to me.

Last night, I spent the night in the 3rd Floor vacant apartment, in The Baby Dolls, an old abandoned Courtway behind the 534 building. I was sitting on Dontae's Benz like a detective on a steak out, but of course, Dontae had never shown. I knew now that, while I was placing the cake I had for him in the oven, he had already baked one for my man Payne-El. That shit that had gone down over at Big Val's crib was a terrorist attack. I had to admit, I had underestimated the young nigga. It wouldn't happen again.

Mi-Mi stirred under the sheets. She moaned groggily, then said, "Where you goin' baby?"

"I gotta go take care of somethin', vic," I told her as I jumped into my jeans. "I'ma double back this way later on."

I sat down on the bed, stepped into my boots, and laced tight.

Mi-Mi turned over, I looked at her. The lil' punk bitch had actually cleaned up well. Her hair was in blue and black box braids. Her nipples and her belly button were pierced. Her mani-pedi had her fingers and toes looking edible. Funny what a lil' scratch can do for even the bummiest bitches.

"Baby," Mi-Mi cooed. "Leave me a couple of dollars fo' you go."

"What's a couple of dollars, vic?"

"Like a hunnid."

I stood up, pulling my black hoodie over my head. "What you need a hunnid dollars for?" I asked her, as I looked her directly in the eye. Bitch ain't gimmie shit to read. Her ass was good.

"I'm tryna pick up some shit from the store."

I knew she was a *pick-up some shit from the store* lie. We had talked about her drug use, which was incomparable to mine, but I still wanted her to stop using. I did enough drugs for both of us. I just didn't want a crack user for my main bitch.

I peeled money for Mi-Mi. Tossed a crispy hunnid dolla bill on the bed and told her, "When I come back in this muhfucka that refrigerator better be full of shit."

I walked over to the closet, got strapped up, and walked out of the bedroom.

Outside, the sky was crying soft tears from its grey eyes. The wind had them tears misty as fuck by the time I marched through the Planet Rock section of the projects. Hallway window slammed shut, hallway doors banged closed and locked.

"Oh, mack buddy in the trench, Jo'!" I heard somebody shout.

"Muhfucka gon' put some of that hot shit in you over here, mellow!"

"Reggie Wade out here, y'all!"

"Knock it off!" I yelled. "Y'all hoe ass niggas dead-popped! Ain't no muhfucka tryna take shit over here!"

"Pretty soon you ain't gon' be takin' shit from nowhere!" A voice yelled from somewhere in the Courtway.

A mean grit curled my lips as rage burned my skin. I spun around as I walked through the empty courtyard. After seeing no sign of the speaker, I yelled, "Bring yo' tough-ass out here and say that shit in my face!" I foamed at the mouth. "Come on! You bad muhfucka! Come on out here and stand on that shit you talkin'!" I said, then I stopped in the center of the Courtyard, arms out, the beast at my thigh.

I was begging for a gunfight. A gunslinger always begged for a fight, and I was a gunslinger, one of the coldest, if not the coldest around here.

"Save that shit for Dontae nem, dope fiend ass nigga! You gon' need it!"

I upped The Beast.

Boom!

The blast echoed in the quiet afternoon air. Birds squawked and flew from their perches in nearby trees. A car alarm sounded off up the street.

"Bitch ass nigga! That's what I got for Dontae nem!" I screamed. "Or any other muhfucka with heart to get in my way!"

I stood there for a moment listening, it was crickets, muhfuckas always had a lot to say on the indirect side, but whenever you made their bitch asses put an address on that shit, they curled up in the fetal. Best place for 'em.

I turned around and leaned back into my march through the projects. I needed to see a man about a dog before I went to war with Dontae.

****

The sky had sucked up its tears by the time I walked down the steps of a three-flat, brick building on 40th and Langley Street. The small lawn in front of the building had a pathway through it that had been tracked down by constant traffic. The stairs to the basement were cracked. The front porch was a tough muhfucka cause it had been beaten down for years and the drain in front of the basement door was so full of yellow, brown, and red leaves that it was backing up. I stepped into a murky puddle and knocked at the wooden, basement door.

I was still knocking when a gruff voice boomed through the door, "Who the fuck is it?"

"It's me, vic!" I shouted through the door. "You know we don't say names. Open this muhfucka up!" I listened for a reply.

Heavy footfalls came toward the door, they sounded like a prison extraction team. For a moment, I felt like I'd be maced in the face, and rushed by big, country white boys in riot gear. I looked up, saw an eye in the peephole. After that, the door broke down like an old hunting rifle and swung into the basement apartments. The nigga that replaced the door was a good stand-in for it. He had shoulders like medicine balls and hands like dump truck shovels. His chest, arms, and thighs had to have been carved out of rock, and they put stupid stress on his wife beater and fatigue pants. Stretcher had been in and out of jail since we were shorties. He hadn't done a year in the street since grade school. But whenever he was out, I knew exactly where to find him in the basement apartment of his mother's building.

He cast a wary glance at me. "What you want, skin and bones?"

"Got damn!" I said with a smile as counterfeited as a three-dollar bill.

I had some rocking to do in this situation. Stretcher had shot Sky and he knew, even though he was gang, me and Sky had been way more jammed than me and him. Rocking him to sleep wouldn't be easy, but it could be done.

Stretcher was a big muhfucka, but he didn't have the sense God gave grapes. "What the fuck? I continued, "Did I burn bridges before I went to the joint, or somethin'? Last time I checked me and you wasn't on this kinda reception?"

"Once upon a time, we was back around this muhfucka, vic." I held my arms out, with my smile still counterfeit. "What happened? It's me—Reg, Black...skin and bones, baby. Dirty Snatchers for life."

Stretcher looked at me good. The eye stayed leery, careful even. He was a dog that didn't wag its tail. I didn't know what to expect from him. He was probably feeling the same way about me.

After a few moments, the ice cracked between us. He stepped aside and said, "Come on in, skin and bones."

I walked past him, into his basement apartment, and he kept his eye on me the whole time. The place was all cement and concrete. It woulda resembled a safehouse for holding kidnap victims, but there was a huge maroon leather sectional, a 60 inch TV, and a Tecnic stereo system. The rest of the joint was all pipes and beams, and the kitchen area was sectioned off from everything else by a wooden partition with Chinese writing all over it.

I walked closer to the sofa, and over it back, I spotted two naked bitches. One had skin like hot caramel, the other had a complexion closer to pecan. Both had huge titties and fat asses. They was curled up under one another, watching The Mack. The movie was at the part where Max Julian meets the blind man.

Stretcher bought his heavy foot ass over. "You bitches get the fuck up and go in the bedroom," he roared. "Can't y'all see I got company?"

Caramel and Pecan became untangled, rolled off the sofa, and tiptoed quickly out of the area with their asses and titties jiggling.

When they disappeared behind the sheet that Stretcher had called the bedroom, I wanted to go with them.

"Have a seat, skin, and bones."

Stretcher pointed toward the sofa and I sat down where the bitches had just left. The spot was still warm. Stretcher sat down in the armchair across from me.

I told Stretcher, "I ain't gon' hold you up, vic. I need your help. I know you heard about what happened to Sky, Baldy, Custom Fit, and Payne-El?"

Stretcher ran his large hand over his bald head, then he brought that hand down over his face and his thick beard. "Yeah, that shit crazy, skin and bones. They was all my nigga, but I know you heard about what happened between me and Sky?"

"I heard, vic, but I only heard the shit from one side," the lie was a small one.

Sky had never told me anything more than that Stretcher had popped him up. I just wanted to hear Stretcher's side of the story. It didn't matter to me either way. I was splitting his wig regardless.

"Shit changed a lot while you was in the box, skin, and bones," Stretcher told me. "We ain't kids no more, roadie. Nigga been out here fallin' in love with that glass dick, and shit. The nigga Sky got so thirsty he broke in my crib and beat me for all my straps and ammo, and shit. I'd cut into him about the shit. He even helped me ride around lookin' for the niggas who did it. I didn't find out he was behind the shit till he sold an AK to one of these shorties around here. Guess how much he sold the shit to him for, skin and bones?"

"How much?"

He placed his forearms on his thigh. A salty look came over his face. His big hands hung between his legs like they were too big for his wrist. "He sold that gun for ten rocks, skin, and bones," he groaned. "Ten stankin' ass dime bags. Now, wasn't that some buzzard ass shit? I tried to kill that nigga, skin, and bones. You woulda reacted the same way."

I told him, "He was definitely outta pocket for that scurvy ass shit," I agreed with Stretcher on the outside, but on the inside, I was bubbling to a boil. Stretcher had shot Sky eleven times. There was no excuse he could give me to justify that shit. He was in violation.

"That nigga was so high off crack he ain't feel not one of them bullets, skin, and bones," Stretcher said as he shook his head.

I crossed my legs T-style and fired up a square. I needed the nicotine to keep me calm. I felt like snatching the nigga Stretcher's soul out through his mouth and delivering it to hell on a trash can lid.

Pussy muhfucka.

"I went by and saw Sky before he got killed, Stretcher," I said, picking lint off my trench coat. "One nigga was in bad shape. He was smokin' out of the can. Broke my heart, he wasn't himself no more, Stretcher. But he was still a Dirty Snatcher."

Stretcher nodded his agreement. His face got softer, he told me, "You're right, skin and bones. I was glad he didn't die. I went by and 'pologized to him and everything. It wasn't no love lost."

I listened to Stretcher's bullshit excuses and decided it'd be best to turn the page on this shit for now. But I made the mental note to revisit the conversation when The Beast was to his head, and my finger was on the trigger.

I told Stretcher, "Them lil' GDs from over there in the body bag buildings popped him and threw him out of the sixth-floor window, Stretcher. I ain't lettin' that shit ride. I can't, cause I'm responsible for that shit, Stretcher. Sky's death is on me."

I told him about my visit to Sky's crib. I told him about the young nigga that had seen me walking out of his joint. I told him about the robbery, the murder, the warning I'd received from the fat boy before I'd sent his soul floating through the ethers.

Stretcher fired up a square. He smoked holding onto the filter like a joint roach. As he puffed at his square, he looked into my eyes like he was still tryna figure out what angle I was coming at him from.

He told me, "Shorty 'nem some lil' demons, skin and bones. Sky ain't tell you?"

"He tried to, Stretcher," I told him as I smashed my square out in the ashtray on the cocktail table. "But you know me, I'm hard at listenin'."

"You mean hard of hearin'?"

"That, too," I said, then reached into my trench coat and pulled out all the dope bundles I'd taken. Well, okay not all of 'em, but I took out what was left of them after I'd snorted for weeks. I sat the shit on the cocktail table.

The dope caught Stretcher's attention.

I told him, "I heard you been gettin' down on the dime blows over there in The Bungalows."

The Bungalows was a small project on 40th and Cottage Grove.

"All I need is for you to pop this shit off for me. I'll buss it up right down in the middle with you, Vic. No felony favors."

Stretcher smashed his square out in the ashtray on the end table. Then he got a look on his face that said he was considering my offer. During our lapse in conversation, I heard one of the bitches in the bedroom moan.

Stretcher snapped, "You bitches cut that shit out over there while I got company!" After he said that, his attention came back to me. "Bet that shit up, skin and bones," he said.

"Leave the shit here. I'll take care of it," I told him. "It's just one more thing, Vic."

"What's that?"

"I need an advance on some of the scratch," I told him. "I'ma about to get to war and if I'm about to do that, I need ammo." I smiled.

Stretcher smiled. "You got some shit with you, skin and bones. I see you ain't change one bit. Welcome home."

Getting an advance of $2500, I left Stretcher's crib and footed it down to 46th and Vincennes, where I jumped in a Jet Livery, which was nothing but another dope fiend with a lil' piece of car, sitting outside of a taxi, dispatch office, taking the rides in neighborhoods. Yellow taxis didn't service out of fear of being robbed, or killed, or both. I'd taken the Jet Livery out to Oak Lawn a small part of the city's Southwest side. Out there, a gun shop and a shooting range sat a couple blocks West of Evergreen Plaza. I know a whiteboy named Striker who worked there. I'd met him in the joint. He'd been in for an arson he'd caught tryna pull an insurance fraud. He loved good dope, and his daddy just so happened to run one of the most popular spots in the city for gun freaks.

I told the cabbie, "Hang tight, vic. I'ma go inside a while. Then, I want you to drop me off on thirty-ninth Street."

The cabbie an old nigga who resembled Redd Fox, told me, "As long as you payin', I'm staying, young blood."

I climbed out of the passenger's side of the blue' 86 Pontiac Parisienne and closed the passenger door behind me. I didn't dwell too much on the area. All I knew was that it was so clean it looked like it belonged in another city.

Guns R Us was a small, standalone storefront beside a trailer and a Dairy Queen. I pulled its glass entrance door open, walked inside, and immediately I was surrounded by semi-automatic rifles, shotguns, and all kinds of accessories. A glass display case ran around the showcase floor in an uneven rectangle. Inside the case, there was every handgun made in the last century. I looked around and spotted Striker in the back of the gun store, behind a section of the glass display case, with a customer, who was a white man that looked like Tom Hanks. He was bald, had a beer gut, and wore a leather biker vest, ripped jeans, and Doc Martin boots.

I walked to the back of the store. Stricker spotted me and lost his shit.

"Fuck," he said. "Reggie-Fuckin'-Wade. Fuck. Shit. Motherfucker."

Striker was a bulky, white muhfucka with too much forehead and thinning brunette hair that he greased and brushed to the side to give off the illusion that he still had a head full of hair. Little did he know, that shit wasn't working. The last nigga to know he was losing hair was always the nigga losing his hair.

I said, "What's up, buddy?"

He told me to give him a minute.

I did that.

Striker rambled on about grains, calibers, ammunition. He was a certified gun freak. The customer's head was spinning by the time he was done with him. He sent him up front to close the sale, then he turned his attention to me.

"Reggie-Fuckin'-Wade. Shit. Fuck. Motherfucker. Sonofabitch," he said every cuss word in the sailor's dictionary.

I told him, "Didn't I tell you I'd come and check you out, vic?"

"You sure fuckin' did motherfucker. Shit. Sonofabitch." He waved me around the glass display case. "Bring your fuckin' ass back here, motherfucker. Shit. Sonofabitch."

I walked through the little wooden swing door and Striker gave me a solid shake and pulled me in for a strong hug. When he finally let me go, he walked off and waved me along. "Come on back here, motherfucker. Shit. Sonofabitch. Reggie-Fuckin-Wade. Fuck. Shit."

I followed Striker through a dim hallway, around a corner, through what looked like a stock room, and into a windowless room with a metal desk, a couple of swiveled chairs, a 16-gallon fish tank full of murky water, and a small collection of whiskey on an oak shelf.

Striker grabbed a bottle of Johnny Walker Red down from the shelf, took a seat behind the desk, and told me, "Have a seat, motherfucker."

I took a seat as Striker opened a drawer behind the desk, pulled out two styrofoam cups, sat them on the desk, and poured us up two.

We toasted to freedom and sloshed a cup back. Striker poured us up again. I told myself I wasn't about to let this fuckin' whiteboy get me sloppy in here.

I told him, "I got somethin' good for you."

Striker smiled and rubbed his palms together. "Let's see what you got, motherfucker."

I fished a bundle of dope out, open it up, pulled out a few bags, and emptied them on the desk.

I gave Striker the first snort. He took a line up each nostril, pinched his nose, and held his head back. "Oh, Reggie-fuckin-Wade. Shit. Fuck. This is some good fuckin' shit here. Whadda ya want for it?"

"I just need some ammo."

I walked out of Guns R Us with enough ammunition to pull a raid on an Army Brigade. When I got back out to the Pontiac, the cabbie was knocked out behind the wheel. He came to when I snatched the door and slammed it shut.

"Where to now, young blood?" he asked.

I told him, "The Ida B. Wells."

****

"If you stickin' up in The Wells, it ain't safe for you out here! I got enough guns and bullets. I'll kill 'till blood floods the drains around this muhfucka!" Big Val Cherry was giving me the rundown on what happened around her way last night.

I had run into her up on 38th Street, right off Vincennes. Her ass was looking a mess, too, in a dingy, pink bubble coat and bent up white Reeboks. Them Reeboks were leaning so hard to the side, they looked like they would give.

"So, that's what the lil' muhfucka Dontae said, huh?" I said chewing on the rocks on my jaws.

Big Val rocked from side to side. "And that ain't all he said, Reggie."

I pulled out a square and a lighter, then I cupped a hand over the end of the fire and the tip of my square to keep out the wind and fired up. "What else he say?" I asked.

Big Val said, "Short me in that square."

I pulled out my pack and gave her one instead. The traffic vroomed East and West on 39th Street as we stood there, near the bus stop. I lit her up and she told me Dontae had sent me a message in blood.

"Somebody tell that bitch ass nigga Reggie Wade he's next to get his shit bussed."

I scanned the area, cautiously. I was out on Front Street in broad daylight. I'd done a lotta dirt. I had to worry about that shit coming back at me from angles I couldn't predict. The worry made me nervous, I smoked faster.

I asked Big Val, "He said all that, huh?"

She nodded. "Yup, Reggie," she said. "He said all that shit just like that."

Big Val didn't know it, but she was putting the cables on me. All the shit she'd told me about the fire at her house and about Payne-El's murder had me ready to smash a muhfucka.

"That shit was bogus, how them lil' GDs did Payne-El, Reggie," Big Val said, tearing up. "What makes it so bad, he ain't stick a muhfucka up in years."

"I wouldn't give a fuck if he did, Big Val," I growled and smoked. "Them lil' muhfucka still ain't have no business touchin' him. They don' violated. They don' violated bad."

In the last few days, I'd lost Baldy, Custom Fit, and Payne-El, and Sky had been dropped from the 6th Floor window. I had taken major losses. I'm talking major ones that I couldn't let side. The body count was lopsided as a muhfucka. It was time for me to start evening the shit up.

I told Big Val, "Gon' get out of the streets, I'll see you later."

She asked me, "You gon' go to war with Dontae nem, Reggie?"

"Go to war," I commented. "I ain't gotta go to war. I'm already in the middle of one."

I thumped my square to the ground and left Big Val standing there on 39th Street. Dope fiends and crack head parted like the Red Sea as I leaned into my March.

"On Mack buddy ass in the black trench coat!"

"Here comes Reggie Wade, y'all!"

"Don't come through here on no stick-up, Mellow!"

I heard windows shut, I heard doors slam. I heard cars go skrrr! Scary muhfuckas.

"If you scared go to church, Reggie Wade is on the scene and Reggie Wade bouta put in some work."

CHAPTER 29
ANGIE

"Bitch, you can't run script on me. Somebody don' hit that pussy. Yup, whoever hit it, hit it out the park, too. Shole did. Your skin is glowin', and shit? Do I know the lucky man?"

That was Princess being all nosy and shit. About ten minutes ago, she had come in my crib, slopped down on the sofa beside me, and kicked off her $700 Louis Vuitton ankle boots. Now, she was rolling a joint on my table and asking about who I'd fucked. She would lose her mind if I told her the nigga that had hit this pussy was her man. Of course, I'd never tell her that. Not because I was protecting her either. I'd never tell her because it'd ruin my plans for Dontae.

I told Princess, "You don't know him, bitch. He's one of my old pieces from the PCs."

The PCs were short for The Prairie Courts, another housing project on 29th, and King Drive. It was the only project where Princess and I had never met other niggas together, so I decided to shoot that one out there to throw her nosy ass off.

Princess fired up the joint and sat back on my sofa curling one leg under her. "What's his name, bitch? You lyin', all secretive, and shit," she spat like she was frustrated with me.

I thought of a name quick, "Ace, I told her! Dang, nosy, I told you, you don't know him."

Princess got that look in her eyes that told me she was trying to recollect something.

Then she said, "Nall, I don't know him. But Ju-Ju might. You know that nigga Ju-Ju runs all that shit over that way."

Ju-Ju was one of the secrets I held onto for Princess. I only knew about him cause Princess had told me if Dontae ever called me looking for her, or asking if she was with me, I was supposed to cover for her. I had asked her why she was cheating on Dontae, and she told me Dontae did his dirt on the low, so she did hers. Then she described her sex with Ju-Ju. She told me he always sucked on her pussy hole, sucked the lips of her pussy, and fingered her pussy and her ass at the same time.

By the time she'd gotten to how he ate her ass and sucked her toes, the entire crotch area of my panties had gotten soaking wet and rode up between my pussy lips until I thought they'd split my whole body in half. Princess knew how to brag about how good her sex life was. She'd did that shit with Dontae, and for real for real, that was why I'd always thought about giving his ass some pussy. I knew I should've felt bad about that shit, but I didn't. Princess could cheat with Ju-Ju all she wanted. I'd never give up her secrets. I'd just keep Dontae busy for her.

I asked her, "You still fuckin' with that nigga, Ju-Ju?"

Princess passed me the joint. "I have tried to end that shit with Ju-Ju a million times, but I ain't gon' lie that's a nasty nigga, Angie."

If he had as much money as Dontae I'd jump off Dontae's dick and be on Ju-Ju's shit with the quickness. Whenever I call on Ju-Ju he's right there to serve my ass. Dontae is in love with one thing in this world, Angie, and that's money."

I passed the joint back to her. "I don't know, Princess. I think Dontae loves you."

She cocked her head and gave me a dry smile. "Bitch, you better toughen up out here in these streets. You got a son to take care of. As far as me and Dontae...I know he loves me. I love him, too. You see how long we been together. But his love don't stop him from enjoying his life. And if love don't stop him. I ain't lettin' it stop me, either. We still young, bitch. You need to get with the program."

"And what's the program, Princess?"

"Why I gotta spell this out for you. bitch? Get everything you need out here. Everybody playin' for keeps. You need to be playin' for keeps, too."

Princess passed me the joint and immediately began rolling up another as I thought about the shit she'd just told me. I can't lie, even though Princess was kinda heartless, she appeared to be enjoying life more than others. She lived in a plush condo off the lake. She had a brand-new BMW, her jewelry, clothing, and shoe game was one million. She had been to Jamaica, Hawaii, and the Bahamas Island. Playin' for keeps was her motto. She was right, I needed to toughen up. Fatso was dead. Life had to go on. I hit the joint once more and dropped it into the glass ashtray on the cocktail table before it burned my fingers. I hated that shit. How could I be a bad bitch with fingertips that looked like I'd been eating Cheetos?

"Playin' for keep, huh, bitch?" I asked as smoke hallowed around my head.

"Yup, it's time for you to get back in the game, bitch," Princess said, then fired up another joint.

"You're a beautiful girl. A nigga would be lucky to be able to keep you."

Princess was right. The only thing is I doubted she'd be telling me to play for keeps if she knew I was about to play to keep her man.

CHAPTER 30
DETECTIVE STEVEN KNOX

"The Brass is on my ass, Steve. You've had almost ten murders down there in The Ida B. Wells in one month, and you've made no arrests. I don't give a fuck what you gotta do. Get some of this shit solved, or I'm sending the Tact Team down there, and your ass will be on desk duty!" Captain Dick Berne barked at me from behind his messy teakwood desk.

He was a bulky Irishman with white hair, coffee-stained teeth, and skin like tanned leather. He had called me into his small corner office to chew me out for the umpteenth time. He needed to relax. Maybe some liquor and a ten-dollar hooker from up on 47th Street would help him.

"I'm workin' a couple of angles," I told him. "I'm just waitin' for a break in the case, Cap. You know how delicate these gang murders are. Nobody wants to be a witness in the projects."

He was having none of what I'd just said. He pulled out a bottle of JB and poured himself a cup.

"You think I'm some kinda fuckin' screwball, Steve? I worked the streets for thirty years. I know the layout there, and I know how you get shit done. I'm tellin' you! Get the fuck out there and get it done! I don't wanna hear anything besides you got an arrest! You hear me!"

"Yeah, Cap," I told him. "I hear you."

This was why I played dirty in the streets. The clean muhfuckas always tried to squeeze the juice out of turnips. They expected miracles while they sat around in their offices drinking and plotting their way closer and closer to City Hall. While regular detectives like me were in the streets busting our asses in impossible situations and environments.

"If you need some help—" Captain Berne said after sloshing back a shot. "—I'll put the entire district at your disposal. Just get me something, Steve. Get me something I can take back to the Brass to let 'em know we're back in control of this thing."

"Okay, Sir."

I thought about where I was with the murders. Bomb in a Bag. Dontae Kirkpatrick. Reginald Wade. I was on the cusp of busting this thing open, but if I forced the issue, I could end up blowing the entire case.

"Can I go now, Cap?"

"You're dismissed."

I walked out of Captain Berne's office and navigated through the maze of cubicles on the 2nd floor of the precinct. I gazed around at all the officers on desk duty. I could never be one of them-tapping keys on a keyboard, printing arrest warrants, and fishing some other detective's paperwork. A desk job was for the birds.

I walked out into the hallway as beat cops moved past me like landscapes outside the window of a speeding car. Quick steps took me to the elevator. I got there just as it slid open. I stepped into it and stopped when I saw Dee-Dee.

"Hi, Steven."

Dee-Dee, Diedra Phillips was one of those big women that a man just couldn't find a way to avoid. She was Mocha-skinned with pretty brown eyes and titties the size of torpedos. Her entire body was juicy. She swallowed a man whole, and she could throw down in the kitchen. The only problem with her was, she didn't know how to sex without strings attached. She was always trying to make a husband out of me when all I wanted to be was a booty call.

"How you doin', Dee-Dee?" I asked her.

She stepped off the elevator, came toward me batting her lashes, and smiling. "I'm fine, I haven't heard from you lately. Where you been?"

I walked by her and held the elevator door. "I been working a caseload," I told her. "The Ida B. Wells thing."

"Oh, yeah," she said. "The murders. I heard about that. You got any suspects?"

"I'm workin' on 'em now."

"Umph...I'll be glad when you're done workin' on them, so you can work on me."

Just then, Jill came around the corner. I wasn't sure she'd heard Dee-Dee. But she looked at her, then looked at me and said, "Hi, Steve. Am I interrupting something?"

I told her, "No, I was just tellin' Detective Phillips about the case I've been workin' down in The Wells. I was tellin' her I wouldn't mind her helping me if she could keep her mouth shut about it," I said, then looked at Dee-Dee letting her know not to say shit out of pocket around Jill.

"Well," Jill said. "I was headed downstairs. Were you holding the elevator for some reason?"

"No," I told her. "Actually, I was on my way downstairs, too."

"Good. Because I got a couple of things to tell you about your cases."

I turned to Dee-Dee and told her, "Detective Phillips, I'll be in touch. You have a nice day."

"Whatever," she said with a salty look on her face as she turned and walked away.

Me and Jill got onto the elevator. The door slid closed behind us and started descending slowly to the ground floor. But halfway between floors, Jill pulled the red, emergency stop button and the elevator cart came to a jerking stop. Then she looked at me from behind heavy lids, unbuttoned her jeans, and shimmied out of them. She wasn't wearing panties. The sight of her neatly-shaven pussy gave me a stiff dick.

Jill came to me. "Come on, Steve," she whispered. "We only got a couple of minutes."

I unbuckled and unzipped. "Whatever happened to me being patient with you?"

"That was bullshit," she said, pulling my hard dick out of my boxes and fondling it. "I'm a woman. And a woman has needs, too."

I pressed her back against the wall and kissed her until both of us lost our breath. Then I grabbed both her legs in my arms, held her on the wall of the elevator cart, broke the skin of her wet pussy, and stroked at her walls vigorously. She bit my ear and moaned as I stroked her, each thrust faster, harder, and deeper inside her.

"Okay, shit!" she cooed. "That's my spot...right...there."

I held her in place and pounded her spot. The elevator rocked to the beat of our rhythm. I thought it would break and we'd fall to our deaths. But at the moment I didn't care about anything besides busting my nut.

"Steve?"

"Yeah."

"You like this pussy?"

"Yeah."

"You'll like it even more in a minute."

"Why?"

"I'm...gonna...cum!" she shrieked. "Ooooohhh...shit!"

Suddenly, I felt her walls contract and expand on me as I oozed inside her hot juices. The feeling made me bear down and finish her off forcefully. She trembled and came again as I came grunting huskily, stroking her with uneven thrusts.

"Now what did you...have...to tell me...about my cases?" I asked as I let her legs fall one at a time.

She caught her breath. "All of those shotgun murders was done with the same shotgun."

I'd figured as much, it was wonderful to have confirmation, though. Dontae was at war with Reggie Wade. I didn't see this ending too well.

CHAPTER 31
DONTAE

"That Ruger you used last night. That was Fatso's shit, wasn't it?"

Cat Eyes asked me about the gun I'd taken from Angie as we stood around the table in the stash house, counting ends. We were getting ready to lay low for a week or two because the law was around this bitch thirsty.

I told him, "Yeah, Angie found it in the closet. She called me to come through and get it cause she didn't feel right havin' in the crib with Rashaun, Jo'."

"Oh, yeah?" he said, shooting me a leery glance.

I kept my eyes on the paper. My story was good enough for him. He didn't need to know that I'd fucked Angie. If he knew that shit, he'd see it like I'd betrayed Fatso. Cat Eyes was loyal like that. Me—not so much.

"Anyways," I said.

"It was just, Kiesha pregnant again and you know we been stayin' in her momma crib. I wanna get us out of there. Think it's time for us to get our own shit."

"Bout time," I told him. "I remember you sayin' how her ole G be goin' in the room stealin' and shit."

"Yeah, I'm sick of that shit. So—"

"Say no more," I told him. "Take a couple of these racks and go ahead and get you and Kiesha a nice trip somewhere."

I looked at Cat Eyes and could see this wasn't about the money. He wanted to say something to me but as usual, he was finding it hard to say whatever it was he was trying to say.

N.W.A's song *Niggas For Life* played in the background. *"It's plain to see/ You can't change me/ 'cause I'ma be a Nigga For Life."*

Cat Eyes leaned back on the stove and said, "A couple of racks ain't gon' cut it, Folk. I ain't lookin' for no more handouts. I got a lot goin' on. I'm tryna open up my own spot."

The words Cat Eyes had just uttered threw me for a loop. Fatso had just been killed. The law was hot on our asses. We were in the middle of a war. Shit! Now, this nigga was ready to strike out on his own and leave me alone to find my way through this shit. Although I didn't want Cat Eyes to roll out on me, I couldn't say that I blamed him. It had been a long time for him on the ground level of things. He had learned the game and besides that, he had grown nigga shit going on in his life. However, I needed him now, I couldn't let him leave.

I told him, "I hear you, Jo'. You sure you ready?"

"I'm about as ready as I'll ever be."

"I gave you ten gees last month and you jagged that shit off," I told him as I began loading the rubberband stacks into the gym bag, on the table. "If you jag ten gees off while you runnin' yo' own shit. It won't be another ten gees comin'. You understand that, don't you?"

I looked at him.

He nodded and said, "I know what this shit hittin' for."

"A'ight, Jo', just gimmie a little time. Let this shit with Reggie Wade play out and blow over, and I'll bless you, on the Gee." I shook up with him.

"A'ight, Folks. That's what it is."

I checked his expression again. He didn't look pleased with my decision.

Without Cat Eyes, I'd have to find someone else less trusted to run the dope lines when Bomb in a Bag got back into the swing of things. This wouldn't be a problem. Sneak was still a little rough around the edges, but I knew how to make a good lieutenant out of him. However, this would take some time. Cat Eyes was probably going to leave 534, but I wasn't ready for him to leave if I had it my way he'd never leave.

Downstairs, we exited the elevator and stepped into the breezy building's lobby. I followed Cat Eyes out of the building onto the front steps. Over at the 510 building dope fiends were crashing the joint like a good party.

Cat Eyes said, "You see that shit, Folks. Weasel 'nem gettin' all that traffic."

"Yeah. Us shuttin' down the best thing that ever happened to that nigga."

"If you think that's somethin', you should see the lines nitty nem gettin'."

Weasel and Frank Nitty were both GDs from the Body Bag building, but that didn't stop us from being competition. Weasel ran a dope bag, he called Toxic, out of the 510 building while Frank Nitty ran some shit called Grove Thang out of the 551 building. Before I'd temporarily shut down Bomb in a Bag, both dope lines had been lucky to eat off the crumbs that fell off my table. Now I was seeing them with lines.

Pool Hall came walking around the corner of the building. "Bossman," he said with his toothpick dangling from his bottom lip. He had a ripped black leather, his black Kangol cap, shit-brown corduroys, and black folks bucks, it was one of his better-dressed days. "You gon' hafta learn to walk and chew bubble gum at the same time."

"Why?" I asked as he walked up the steps. "What's up, old nigga?"

He pulled his toothpick out of his mouth and said, "Piece of wood?" he continued. "That dope Toxic and Groove Thang sellin' is pure-dee-garbage. The onliest reason dope fiends is buyin' it is cause you ain't go yo' thang out here."

"I hear you, old nigga."

"I know you hear me. You too near me not to hear, but is you listenin'?"

I checked. "I'm listenin'. Just gimmie a couple more days, old nigga. I just wanna let things cool off and we gon' get at 'em with a bomb."

"Okay, bossman," Pool Hall said as he turned and shuffled away.

Cat Eyes asked me if I wanted him to give me security to the Benz. I told him I was straight. After that, we shook up and went our separate ways. As I walked away I hiked the strap of the gym bag higher on my shoulder and thought about getting Bomb in a Bag back rolling. Dope fiends were fickle. Their loyalty was only to good dope. I needed to get back to work before they found somewhere else.

CHAPTER 32
REGGIE WADE

As the sun went down, I was in the broken window of a vacant rowhouse apartment, at the end of the 500 block of 37th Street. From where I was, I could see the corner. It was empty except for Dontae's Benz, parked Northway. I was praying for him to appear. This had been the 2nd time I'd had to spend hours in the vaco waiting for him. The whole shit was starting to piss me the fuck off. I wanted to run up in the 534 building, but I knew them shorties in those black coats were strapped. I wasn't looking for a gunfight, I was tryna catch a body.

I pulled out a bag of dope and snorted it out of the bag. When I got that shit up in me I relaxed. I hated this fucking place. This three-bedroom hell had been the place my dope fiend ass momma had raised us. That bitch used to beat the shit out of us with those fucking extension cords and him, he used to—

"What you lookin' at, you lil' freak bitch?" his voice sounded like bald tires over gravel.

I'd stumbled out of me and my brother Ronnie's bedroom half asleep. Muffled cries and screams had woken me up and brought me to my big sister's cracked bedroom door, where I'd found him between Rachel's tiny legs, his hairy ass movin' in and out, his veiny hand over her mouth. A rage kindled to a blaze inside of me, but my feet had stuck to the floor like Velcro.

"You want some of this pussy, too, huh? Come on get you some of this sweet shit, boy. Or is you scared of pussy?" He smelled like cheap liquor. His words came out slurred. I just watched and didn't blink, didn't swallow. He snapped, "What you gon' do—just stand there and watch?"

I cried.

"Oh," he said. "I know what it is. You don't want none of this pussy," he said. "You wanna gimmie some of that ass!"

I shivered. Every hair on my body stood up. A chill ran up and down my spine.

"That's it, bitch boy wanna gimmie some of that tight lil' ass he got."

He snatched his dick out of Rachel, crawled from between her legs, rolled out of bed, and stood there with a yellow discharge leaking from the head of his dick.

"Go 'head, bitch boy, suck that dick. You don't want no pussy. You must be some kinda freak."

Fuck! I shook my head fast and hard and massaged my temples to get rid of the bad memories. He was dead now. Rachel had killed him. Good! He wouldn't hurt nobody, no more. Since the bad memories faded, I turned my attention back to the window. I couldn't have done that shit at a better time because, when I looked out the window again, I saw Dontae. He was wearing a black skully, black leather, black everything. Even the gym bag on his shoulder was black.

"Yeah, muhfucka, I got yo' ass now," I mumbled, seeing that Dontae was a little heavy around the waist. I didn't give a fuck. The element of surprise was with me and niggas in the street didn't take too well to surprises.

I ran out of the Vaco, swinging The Beast up.

Boom!

I pulled the trigger.

Dontae fell, but I couldn't tell if I'd hit him, or not. "I heard you been lookin' for Reggie Wade, vic!" I shouted.

Boom! I pulled the trigger again.

"Niggas don't come lookin' for Reggie Wade! Reggie Wade come lookin' for niggas!"

CHAPTER 33
DONTAE

Boom!

I heard you been lookin' for Reggie Wade, vic!"

Boom!

"Niggas don't come lookin' for Reggie Wade! Reggie Wade come lookin' for niggas!"

The shotgun blasts caught me off guard. I knew I had some buck shots in my leather, maybe even in my hoodie, but I hadn't caught a slug. I'd hid my head just in the nick of time. A sudden burst of adrenaline raced through my heart. I snatched both of my .40s out, clicked 'em off safety, and rubbed the barrels together.

Car alarms whined loudly up the street.

Boom!

Glass shattered and rained down on me.

My lips curled in anger.

"Where you at, shorty?" Reggie Wade shouted. "Come on out. Stand up and be accounted for. Ain't that the way you cold, brick ass niggas say that shit?"

Boom!

Buck shots peppered the body of the Benz.

Ooh, shit! This bitch ass nigga had got the ups on me. Suddenly, something Streetlight told me came to mind: *"I don't know where you can find him, but I know how. Keep askin' people where you can find him, and he'll find you."*

I had turned over enough rocks. Now, here was the snake, about fifty feet away, lunging at me, tryna bite my head off. I peeped over the trunk of the Benz and spotted Reggie Wade coming toward me.

"I ain't tryna lip box with you, nigga!" I shouted, then popped up like a jack-in-the-box, blowing at his ass over the trunk of the Benz.

Blocka! Blocka! Blocka! Blocka! Blocka! Blocka!

I sent six shots in his direction, he got low and took cover behind the corner of the rowhouse building.

"Uh-uh-uh," he grunted, tryna clown me. "That's what's wrong with you, young niggas. All those guns, all those bullets, no aim!"

"I'll show you aim, nigga!" I shouted. "Come from behind that building!"

Block! Block! Block! Block! Block! Block!

"Yeah, shorty! I'm triple-breasted out here!"

The last shots he sent at me blew the back tire out from under the Benz. It leaned like an old junkie. He was killin' my shit.

Blocka! Blocka! Blocka! Blocka! Blocka! Blocka!

I shot back at his ass, keeping him at bay.

"You missed again, shorty!" he shouted. "Somebody really oughta teach you how to shoot!"

"You come out and teach me, nigga!" I shouted as I popped in more clips.

"I'll teach you, shorty. But after I teach, you ain't gon' be able to use what you learned!"

Boom!

A shotgun blast punctuated his words.

The buck shots sounded like a fisherman casting a net in the river.

Blocka! Blocka! Blocka!

"I ain't buyin' them wolf tickets you sellin', nigga!" I yelled with spit flyin' every which way out of my mouth.

"You better ask a muhfucka 'bout me, shorty! I don't see no wolf tickets!" he shouted. "I Play For Keeps!"

Boom!

Blocka! Blocka! Blocka!

"I did ask muhfuckas about you. And they told me you a dope fiend ass nigga that can't keep his hands out of another nigga's

211

pockets! You ain't out here playin' for keeps! I don't know who you think you foolin'. You out here playin' to get high!"

Blocka! Blocka! Blocka!

Poc! Poc! Poc!

I squatted on my hunches, looked toward the 534 building, and saw Sneak and Lil Tonio running my way. I waved them away, pointed toward the rowhouses. They took off running across the street.

"You know what else they told me?"

"What else they tell you, shorty?"

"They told me yo' momma was a dime bag dope head, your brother is rapist, and yo' stepdaddy used to rough your sister off for the pussy. They also told me, he mighta' even fucked you."

Boom! Poc! Poc! Poc!

Rat! Tat! Tat! Tat! Tat! Tat!

That was Lil' Tonio with the Tech-9. He couldn't wait to blow that bitch.

"Oh, I see you got a lil' help!" Reggie Wade shouted. "I shoulda known you couldn't fuck with me by yourself. You ain't standin' on shit, shorty."

Blocka! Blocka! Blocka!

Rat! Tat! Tat! Tat! Tat!

Poc! Poc! Poc!

After the last volley of shots, I heard sirens.

"You shouldn't have got in my mix, shorty!" Reggie Wade shouted. "When I catch you down bad, I'ma leave yo' lil' ass stankin', vic. That's on me."

"You coulda did that this time, nigga! You was pump fakin'!"

"I don't pump fake, shorty! Ask you fat homie! He tried me and I folded his fat, bitch ass up like a lawn chair!"

Blocka! Blocka! Blocka!

"I don't pump fake either! That Dirty Snatchers count short as a muhfucka 'bout now!"

Boom! Boom! Boom! Boom!

Poc! Poc! Poc!

Blocka! Blocka! Blocka!

Rat! Tat! Tat! Tat!

I told the nigga, "I'ma buss yo' shit when I catch you!"

He told me, "Take a number, shorty! That line is long as the one for hell!"

I heard sirens getting closer. I heard Chevy engines roaring. It was only a matter of time before the twisters showed up. I didn't wanna be on the scene when they did.

"Gon get up outta here, shorty!" Reggie Wade shouted. "I don't want you to get popped. I need you to stay free so I can kill yo' young ass, vic!"

Just then, two bluecoat cars came fishtailing around the corner of 37th and Vincennes, cherries spinning and flashing, tires skidding and screeching, sirens yelling and screaming bloody murder in the crispy air.

I tucked my .40s, stayed low, and took off full speed toward the 534 building.

If me and Reggie Wade had been playin' chess, our first clash would've been called a Stalemate. But we weren't playin' chess, we were Playin' For Keeps and when you play for keeps a stalemate is a loss. Upstairs, from the window of the stash-house, I could see Vincennes Avenue.

The twisters had the Benz yellow-taped off. A bluecoat was sitting red cones down over shell-casings. Dicks was combing the scene for anything. Faggot Steve's ho' ass was pointing at the holes in the Benz. I didn't like that shit. He was already on my bumper, I didn't need him any thirstier to lock me up than he already was. I was wondering when they would leave the scene. As soon as they were gone I would go down and get my ends out the trunk, that wasn't gonna happen.

Minutes later, a tow truck pulled up in front of the car, hooked the Benz up, and carried it away.

Damn! I'd fucked around and left the doors open.

Fifty-two gees in cash was in the truck. I had to get that car back.

To Be Continued

COMING SOON

PLAYIN' FOR KEEPS 2: SCARS FOR SCABS

Made in the USA
Middletown, DE
13 April 2022